Looking towards the [ ]
of the Phalangist lead
over. The stocky man
truck's engine and dr
turned to the right an
centre-piece of the small quadrangle.

The bank lay almost directly opposite the road they had
taken into the square, extending from its right-hand
corner almost to its centre, an imposing frontage of
nearly two hundred feet. The view of the exit road was
obstructed by a statue and a fountain which took up
most of the space in the centre of the square. The
uniform height of the buildings surrounding that road
shut out most of the strong sunlight to give an air of
gloom. In any other circumstances the road would be a
shaded, cool haven, but to Davis it represented anything
but a haven. Swinging the truck around, he stopped,
selected reverse gear and, with Makmoud's aid, reversed
into the gaping hole that had once been an expensive
facade. The wheels bumped over the bodies of the dead
Moslem gunmen, hapless victims of a plot that had little
to do with their religious war. Davis ran the truck back
into the darkened interior until the tailgate was a few
feet from the long mahogany counter. He switched off
the motor.

At last Tippett was able to take the box of grease off his
knees and stretch his long legs.

"We made it," he murmured. And, except for the prone
figure of Crofts, on the floor by their feet, they had. So
far . . .

Hit!
Chris Dempster

CORGI BOOKS
A DIVISION OF TRANSWORLD PUBLISHERS LTD

HIT!

A CORGI BOOK 0 552 12007 3

First publication in Great Britain

PRINTING HISTORY
Corgi edition published 1982

Copyright © Chris Dempster 1982

This book is set in 10/11 Plantin

Corgi Books are published by
Transworld Publishers Ltd.,
Century House, 61–63 Uxbridge Road,
Ealing, London, W5 5SA

Made and printed in Great Britain by
Cox & Wyman Ltd., Reading.

1

On a late Monday evening in the month of September, 1976, Tom Davis was finishing his customary walk across the school playing fields that bracketed together the small town of Camberley and the first wooded slopes of Surrey. Above him, scuffed and raked by a cold northern wind, low masses of thick grey cloud obscured a glassy autumn moon; behind him, the brick silhouette of the school was just visible across a misted acre of trampled grass.

Davis, a powerfully-built, broad-shouldered man in his middle thirties, stopped briefly to pull up the damp collar of his old and weathered combat jacket. He lit a cigarette, cupping the lighter in his palm, and watched his two great dogs chasing shadows across the flat, spongy expanse, before calling them in. It had begun to rain. The wind brought it in gusts like a fine seaspray over a promenade. His hands, dug into his pockets, were stiff with cold.

Some way ahead now, through mist and rain, a row of bright yellow street lamps garishly illuminated a terrace of neat, red brick suburban houses, the symmetry broken here and there by the irregular shapes of more pretentious buildings, gabled and shuttered and lit from below, bringing trees into relief. He set off towards them, feeling the cling of mud under his feet, and the dogs settled easily to his stride, panting, sending out gouts of warm breath. The rain seemed to thicken by the moment. It sprayed off the tarmac and glistened under the lamps.

He turned right out of the rusted, difficult iron gate and

made his way down the deserted street, noticing blue television lights behind certain curtained windows, watching brighter ones snap on suddenly in upstairs rooms. A car went past quickly, sluicing water, but no-one else was braving the cold, wet, prematurely wintry evening.

Davis dropped the butt of the cigarette into the gutter and paused again, having seen something: the bright gleam of tail lights and the stationary car. The Great Dane saw it too and instinctively the short hair between his shoulders rose and the lolling, pink tongue disappeared. Somewhere in that great cavernous chest a growl made its beginnings, but died abruptly when the man murmured to the big dog and touched its massive head reassuringly. The car was parked, with careful deliberation, across the bottom of his drive, but still too far away to identify. He walked on slowly, scanning both pavements, until the numbers on the yellow plate had clarified, then he pushed past the Scimitar and opened the house door, letting the dogs loose into the unlit hallway. Retracing his steps, he rapped his knuckles against the driver's window. The misted glass rolled down obediently.

"Social call?"

The sallow, pock-marked face at the open window looked back without expression, as if resenting the familiar note. Beyond him in the passenger seat, another and smaller man, hunched inside a bulky tan overcoat with its fur collar turned up, inclined his head in a brief, formal greeting. His name was Michael Christie. Davis knew him slightly and had met him on four or five previous occasions. Each time, Christie had been offering work, and twice Davis had accepted the commission. There was only one reason why he should have turned up again.

"We've come to see if you're interested in a spot of late supper," the driver said finally, tapping the steering wheel with a long, ringed finger in apparent impatience.

Davis shrugged dismissively.

"Where?"

There was a pause.

"The Hilton."

The information failed to surprise him although his faint, amused smile seemed to query it. He rested a hand against the car's wet, lamplit roof and leaned further forward.

"When?"

"Half an hour." The ringed finger resumed its listless tapping. Davis hesitated. He looked back over his shoulder, through the rain, towards the dark silent house promising a familiar if unremarkable comfort. His reverie was interrupted sharply.

"Davis! The Hilton ain't in Camberley."

He turned round slowly, acknowledging the rebuke with a broader, franker grin, conscious of the rain dripping from his nose and chin. The car radio was softly playing some maudlin orchestral melody, filling the smokey interior with the lush candences of violins. It struck him as odd and out of place. It reminded him, strangely, of sentimental and emotional attachments that ought to have kept him in place, but never did. He removed his hand from the shining, fibre-glass car roof.

"I've got to change," he said abruptly. "I'll be with you."

"We'll wait then," Christie replied quietly, looking away.

He reappeared about five minutes later in clean denims, freshly shaved with pieces of toilet tissue stuck on some bloody spots on his chin. They left Camberley, went through Bagshot, and within four minutes of Davis climbing into the car, they were on the M3 heading into London.

The Scimitar sped easily through the light traffic on the London-bound motorway, the windscreen wipers battling against the torrential rain storm. The sound of their steady, monotonous clacking together with the crackling of the radio inhibited conversation, though occasionally the two men in front exchanged desultory comments or played with the radio controls. They showed no inclination to brief Davis any further, leaving him to stare quietly out of the small side window at the passing headlights, but it was not something he expected anyway.

He closed his eyes and realised that he felt tired. A sceptical and pragmatic man, experience had left him with very few illusions about the nature of these late night antics. There had been many such assignations during the course of the last few years: meetings with unremarkable or self-important men in anonymous hotel lobbies, hastily organised, vainly, disappointingly or treacherously concluded. Some of these men had unveiled schemes of such ludicrous impracticality that it brought their sanity into question. Others, the petty clerks of governments in exile, the handmaidens of deposed rulers or commercial companies, appeared on the scene one day, carrying attaché cases stuffed with crisp new bank notes, only to disappear the next, like conjurers' apprentices. It was, after all, Davis sometimes reflected, a world of illusions, of fantastic schemes, bizarre plots, just as much as a world, hidden from plain sight, of military coups, political struggles and real events.

But promising lucrative adventures, these anonymous, shadowy figures always found a small and ready audience of men who were well-trained, bored and anxious to escape the ordinariness of peace and civilian occupations. Davis himself, an ex-paratrooper, a veteran of three wars, including Cambodia and Angola, knew all about such emotions and the low threshhold of boredom which made men willing volunteers for wars in which they had no personal interest, but he had almost had a gut full. Frustration and disappointment had made him pessimistic. He was not tired of being a mercenary, but increasingly tired of the mercenary scene. He disliked many of the people who, after Angola, had muscled or bought their way into it, and he distrusted their motives and expertise. For, at bottom, he still liked to regard himself as a soldier. There was something clean, decent and simple about the actual, practical business of war, whatever the continent or cause, so he resented those men whose personal ambition and greed complicated and cheapened the profession.

Davis, suppressing a yawn, lit a cigarette and tried to stretch out his cramped legs beneath the seat. They were already beyond the outskirts of Richmond and the traffic had thickened, magnetised by the metropolis. He could, at least, take some comfort from the presence of Christie whose reputation as a recruiter of men and arms, though almost inevitably tarnished, had at least been established over many years. Christie had been behind the British mercenary expeditions to Nigeria, Cambodia, Angola and, lately, Rhodesia. He had also been involved in a number of unprofitable, abortive coups, mostly directed against tiny independent states that were difficult to detect on any ordinary maps, had probably been responsible for over a dozen assasination contracts, and was now largely regarded as one of the principle English contacts in the illicit but flourishing arms trade. Consequently he was a central, pivotal figure in the subterranean world of mercenary politics, and yet, in truth, he appeared an unlikely candidate for such a position. Small, sharp-featured, reticent, humourless and ill at ease in company, he was a solitary, unforceful and vaguely furtive character about whose own past little was known and even less given away. He had almost certainly served at some point with the British army, but where and in what capacity, whether as paratrooper or, most likely, as a mess cook, no-one could be certain. Later he had formed his own road haulage company, which had wound up in the bankruptcy courts three years later, and somehow, during that time or later, had come into personal contact with Mike Hoare, the mercenary leader. He had worked assiduously after that cultivating the right contacts and manipulating the right people in high circles and low, eventually to emerge as the man with the greatest facility for organizing the transportation of men and arms around the world. Doubtless, at this stage, his mercurial habits, his ability to go to ground without a trace then reappear at the propitious moments gave him an advantage over others in the field, like Delaney and Moore, who courted publicity and attention. These, after all, were attractive qualities to those who required a job done quietly and efficiently. They were not, however, attractive qualities as far as Davis was concerned, and he was no more inclined to trust Christie than he was any other natural predator. Nevertheless

9

he was well aware that, with Christie around, something interesting, possibly genuine, and hopefully lucrative was in the air. He would make his own mind up later, after hearing the proposition, but for the moment, since his life had once again grown stale, Davis was perfectly prepared to go along for the ride.

He noticed, outside the car, the first warm clustering lights of the city, reflected on the wet and greasy roads in dabs of muted colours, like some abstract modern painting. He lit a fifth cigarette and listened to the subdued conversation between the others, eventually making out the punch line of some crude, familiar joke. He remembered hearing it first in a mud hut, in a small village composed of similar mud dwellings, in Angola. At the time he was picking metal splinters out of the back of a man's leg, from a wound the size of his own fist. The man, delirious from pain and morphine, had told jokes in his moments of lucidity, and during the four long hours of suffering and care a bond had developed between the two men. Later, it had helped them to survive the madness and butchery of Colonel Callan's régime, and return to England alive.

The wounded man's name was Daniel, or Danny, Tippett, the driver of the car. He was a tall, thin, black-haired and strikingly handsome man with more than a taste for the good things in life, especially women. Habitually well-dressed — in distinct counter to Davis's bleached jeans and flying jacket — softly spoken, his voice having almost entirely lost its earlier traces of an East End childhood, Tippett looked and sounded anything but a professional mercenary even though he, too, had already fought in three wars and on two continents, where his reputation as an explosives expert had been confirmed.

Like many mercenaries, Tippett had come from a military background although, unlike most, he had never been in the army. His father, a professional soldier for most of his life, and often absent from the family home had only passively encouraged his son to enlist, and Tippett, even as a young man, had been attracted to more lucrative occupations. After a few years of doing little but assess his opportunities, he had finally decided on safe-blowing and armed robbery, and despite the six years spent in Wormwood Scrubs as a result, he had never looked back with regret on the decision. It had taught him a valuable skill, and it had toughened his spirit. For despite his prepossessing appearance and pleasantly dry humour Tippett was a hard, ruthless and arrogant character with an inclination to violence which sometimes surprised Davis. Indeed at first the two men, prompted by mutual distrust, had avoided one another, while Davis at least had attempted to understand this strangely divided personality. In the end, the wound had broken down the stiff, awkward barriers between them, and Davis had given up his psychology.

They were now in Knightsbridge, and Tippett pointed to Harrods as they swept past it, taking the lights at amber.

Davis leaned forward between the seats and looked across at Christie.

"Give me a name."

Christie didn't bother to turn his head, smothered as it was in the dark thick fur of his collar.

"His name is Martin Hoffman, and all he said was this: could I come tonight for supper bringing an explosives expert and a small arms and vehicle expert and talk about the Middle East, 'vault doors, the PLO, and a lot of money — expenses paid, of course.' "

The third member of the trio, Tippett, suddenly spoke for the first time since Camberley.

"Expenses, that's the first fuckin' time you've mentioned that!"

"Well, it shows that it could be serious," replied Christie. Both the other two men had been on jaunts with Christie before, and had ended up, invariably, out of pocket.

"How much more serious?" enquired Davis.

"I've told you, supper — and a hundred each."

"Pence?" enquired Tippett sarcastically.

"If that's all you want, I'll keep the other ninety-nine quid," countered Christie sourly.

"Just what have we to do for these expenses?" said Davis.

11

"All he wants us to do is to listen to a proposition. If we don't like it, or don't want to get involved, we just eat the man's food, drink a little wine, take his screwing money and leg it — OK?"

Nothing more was said until they pulled out of Park Lane and Tippett remarked that they'd arrived.

The Scimitar pulled in front of the hotel's entrance, which was bathed in spotlights. Davis climbed out slowly, observing for a few seconds the human freight passing through the great glass doors. He ground out the butt of the cigarette with his heel.

"Rich bastards," he said softly, before moving away.

Martin Hoffman had arrived in London two days earlier from New York by courtesy of a British Airways Concorde. It was his third visit in as many months and, as before, he avoided the fashionable hotels and took possession of a well-appointed and roomy flat overlooking the gardens in Hans Place, Knightsbridge which was always at his disposal. He preferred a certain amount of privacy and seclusion and disliked the thought of sleeping in a small, impersonal hutch in a crowded warren. In any case he found it easier to entertain women at the flat. Women were a luxury he could well afford, and though in truth he frequently found their company and conversation stultifying and irksome, he also took a certain pleasure in collecting them, rather in the way he collected modern paintings and ornate pieces of French furniture. As a connoiseur of both he always knew what object he was looking for, and invariably found it.

It was rumoured that Hoffman had not always enjoyed the privileges of affluence; that his background had been humble, provincial and unpromising. Like so much else about the man, however, the rumours were hard to substantiate, but neither did they interfere with his astonishingly rapid and celebrated rise to a position of comparative prominence on Wall Street, as they might have done in any country other than America. From a distance, Hoffman's emergence from obscurity to prominence in a matter of some three years was, for a number of

Americans, especially those ambitious politicians anxious for a friend in the financial and banking fraternity, exemplary of the American Dream. The poverty from which he came merely added lustre to an attractively elusive, charismatic figure, and even if Hoffman had propagated the myth in the first place he was now in no position to dispel it, even had he wanted to.

Hoffman's actual position was never fully explained or revealed, though it was widely thought that he acted as advisor to a number of financial institutions, including banks like the American Bank of Miami, and several large corporations. It was known that he had a controlling interest in two small, New York based computer companies with heavy trading commitments in Israel, and there had recently been some speculation of political ambition or even a White House appointment, again in an advisory capacity to the Treasury. However much he might deny such speculations, they persisted, and yet the irony remained that Hoffman himself was well known in only a few, higher circles. He was not a public figure. He was not even resident in America for more than two, perhaps three months a year. The house in London was only one of many, and perhaps in a sonse he no longer belonged to any country or felt any real social attachments. At the age of thirty-nine he already belonged to that small, elite class of financially and socially independent people who share the world out between them.

Nevertheless he was an uncharacteristic member of that class because he failed to share its indolent and cultured pursuits. He could rarely relax, and never permitted himself the luxury of even a short holiday. His ethic was work. Within a few hours of his arrival in Hans Place he had put through calls to New York, Boston, Washington, Miami, Geneva and two to Beirut. He had arranged several meetings, for the next day and the day after in London, though only one in the City, and had alerted his Saville Row tailor to an imminent visit. Finally, before going to bed that night, he had called his assistant, Robert Sneiger, in Paris. Sneiger had answered the phone with

13

typical promptitude, for Hoffman never employed those who expressed any reluctance to work on his behalf day and night. He paid them well and he expected unquestioning loyalty and commitment. What Hoffman couldn't know was that Sneiger answered from his bedroom and not his study. Nor could he see the face of the young Frenchman looking up from Sneiger's crumpled pillow as the older man rolled away and snatched the receiver. On the other hand, embarrassingly for Sneiger, he would not have been at all surprised.

"Yes?"

"Robert?"

"Yes, Martin. Just a moment." Sneiger slid his legs out from beneath the thin sheets and sat up, picking up his spectacles with his free hand. "Go ahead."

"I want you here by tomorrow afternoon. About four," Hoffman snapped.

"Okay. Where are you?"

"Hans Place."

The proximity of London allowed Sneiger a sense of relief. "About four. I'll be there."

"Good," Hoffman said, and replaced the phone.

By the time Sneiger's plane touched down at Heathrow, Hoffman had already completed much of his work. An early trip to Saville Row had been followed by an hour spent contemplating the map, large enough almost to cover the mahogany table in the flat's dining room, and the file of index cards, each separate card containing a single, personal biography, each the result of Sneiger's painstaking research. At three o'clock, Hoffman had a second and final conversation with Michael Christie, arranging to meet him the following evening in the foyer of the Hilton hotel. He suggested that Christie might like to bring along a couple of friends, and proposed Tippett and, possibly, Tom Davis, who he had heard was a good car mechanic. The mercenary had agreed to contact both, and thought it more than likely they would find the time to meet the American banker.

"Excellent," Hoffman had finished. "Tomorrow night at

ten, then. I'm sorry this is at such short notice."

"Sometimes it can't be helped," Christie agreed. "I'm sure we can fix something up."

"I was relying on that," Hoffman had said with obvious conviction.

Sneiger arrived twenty minutes later, a slim, narow-shouldered, precise figure with a black English umbrella tucked under his arm and wearing a long, dark blue, French looking raincoat: an indication, to the oblivious Hoffman, that the weather had changed outside from the morning's pale and watery sunshine to thick, grey, mutinous clouds threatening rain.

Sneiger removed the raincoat, hanging it fastidiously behind the door. As Hoffman had noticed on previous occasions, he was meticulously careful about appearances, even fussy, to the point where his vanity seemed incongruous. Appearances mislead, of course, and there was a toughness — at least intellectual toughness — behind the man's apparent delicacy, his mannered gestures. Indeed Hoffman had noticed it at once, when he had enticed him away from another and much more respectable walk of life and put him to his work. Sneiger, with his pinched, vaguely rodent-like face with its colourless eyes and mousy, swept-back hair, had proved more than an effective backroom operator — he had proved himself shrewd, political, dispassionately intelligent. There was no love lost between them, and probably little real respect, but then Hoffman was paying good money for reliable service and unquestioned obedience. He felt confident that Sneiger hadn't the imagination to be ambitious, and in any case experience had taught him the value of employing someone whose weaknesses and vanities were visible and accessible. In an operation of this sort, naturally, the vanities would count against him, the weaknesses would be exposed. But, then, realistically, it hadn't been Hoffman's choice. Sneiger had more or less (the politics were as ever cloudy, ambiguous, problematic) been co-opted, detailed to participate. No one expected Hoffman himself to contribute, to put himself at personal risk, but

15

nevertheless he was left responsible, accountable, and there was nobody else, when it came down to it, that he could trust, even if, ironically, he trusted Sneiger miserably little.

The two Americans, settling down to business, were oblivious to the rain splashing, spattering against the wide windows as they went through each step of the plan carefully, making constant references to the marked map on the table and the file of cards.

After two solid hours of work Hoffman produced a bottle of Jack Daniels and two glasses. It made a pretence of relaxation. For a moment he watched Sneiger rinse the liquid round his mouth, as if he were tasting expensive wine. Then he said quietly,

"I'm sorry you have to go with them on this."

The other returned his glance patiently and with deliberate care, before replying.

"My choice."

Hoffman shrugged.

"Sure," and paused. "But I didn't mean that. I mean it might jeopardise things. I don't know how you'll react."

"It was my choice," Sneiger repeated. "All right?"

"Some things we don't have much control over."

"So . . . . what do you expect me to say?" The colourless, greyish eyes, obdurate, gave nothing away.

"Nothing." No choice. Hoffman tapped his fingers against the polished wood. "What else?"

Sneiger, swallowing another mouthful of bourbon, knew how pessimism would be interpreted. He toyed with his words, delivering them thoughtfully. After all it was necessary to have reservations.

"If you want to know, my real concern is the time factor. Something like this . . ." opening his hands out, pausing. "Something like this should be planned over two, three months. We've got three weeks. Maybe less. That effectively means we have to rely a great deal, perhaps too much, on others, like Christie for example, to arrange and organise things for us. It makes us vulnerable. It makes . . . If we just

16

had, say, another month. Just another few weeks, for God's sake . . ."

"But we don't," Hoffman interrupted sharply, annoyed. "The timing is not of our choosing. You know damn well that's the whole point. The only thing we can't organise or predict is what happens out there, in the real world. You know, the news! Sure, some people, especially some people, think everything's planned, orchestrated . . . bullshit! Now, anything else, constructive, you can think of?"

Sneiger, wincing, took out a handkerchief and patted his cheeks. His dislike of Hoffman was something tangible, as hard and firm as a clenched, cold piece of metal.

"I think I ought to meet them in Cyprus," he offered at last, putting the cloth away, his hands flat on the table, fingers touching the smooth glass.

"Why?"

"More opportunity to brief them. It's also important that they get to know me before we go in. They'll take less notice of a familiar face."

"Agreed," Hoffman said. "Exactly one week from today you'll meet up with them in Larnaka. You know the hotels?"

Sneiger nodded. He knew the whole elaborately simple plot, every twist and turn. So much of it was his. He knew more than Hoffman. That was the only satisfaction. Hoffman . . .

"Anything else?" Hoffman prompted.

So many other things, Sneiger thought, suppressing a smile, looking away pensively towards the window, misted now. A different ending, for one.

"Passport? Those — what are they? — documents for the port auth . . ."

"Everything's arranged," Sneiger told him curtly, "Or will be in a week. I'll keep you informed."

."Naturally."

"And Chamoun?"

"He'll send someone over to rendezvous at the hotel, and

17

arrange the boat. Then, God knows, a charabanc to Beirut. Something . . ."

"Okay. What about getting out? Want me on the boat?"

"I told you. Your job. Those boxes are your responsibility. Fuck the rest."

"Yeah. The boxes."

Hoffman stood up, scraping the chair, unmistakably irritated.

"I don't think you should express any opinion on that."

"I wasn't going to. It's nothing to do with me. I'm not a curious person. Listen, I don't care."

"Good. That's right. Haven't you a plane to catch?"

Sneiger, obliged to stand up, did so slowly, brushing the creases out of his jacket with a slim hand. Hoffman watched him.

"One thing," Sneiger said, without reluctance. "It's not watertight. It's chancy. There's a big, big risk . . . I'm not complaining. It's all right. It might work. But just so we both know . . ."

"Of course." Hoffman frowned, almost petulantly, then went on, "You know Lindquist is in Paris?" He produced a small, gold rimmed card from his wallet. "This is his address. I want him here tomorrow. Friday at the latest. He's expecting you to call. Well, goodbye, Robert."

Sneiger collected his raincoat and umbrella. He didn't have a case. He opened the first door.

"Oh, Robert," Hoffman said, following him out. "I don't have to worry about your moral feelings over this, do I?"

For a second it confused and puzzled Sneiger, seemed to indicate an unexpected knowledge. But did it? He couldn't find out, couldn't press, without giving himself away. He looked back upon those cold, pitiless blue eyes and shook his head.

"No. Not at all."

"Good. I am glad," and Hoffman closed the door behind his departing assistant. He returned to the living room and poured himself another large drink, taking it back with him to the table. The map was ringed in several places. He studied the ringed cities and towns for a moment, picturing them in his mind. One of them was Larnaka, the small Cypriot sea-port. Another was Beirut. He pitched his finger down carefully within the small, red circle, and smiled.

2

The three mercenaries waited for Hoffman, as instructed, in the busy, spacious foyer of the Hilton, watching its predominantly Arab population trail their skirts across the thick pile carpeting like a procession of solemn, incongruous monks. The foyer, with its constant, cosmopolitan human traffic reminded Davis of the terminus to some small, modern airport, but like the others he was familiar enough with it to be a comfortable observer, and he noticed with amusement that Tippett had already renewed an old acquaintance with the blonde receptionist behind the glass desk.

Hoffman arrived exactly on time. When he appeared they saw a tall, broad-shouldered and well-groomed figure, carrying a black attaché case and a confident smile. Even from a distance he made an impression of vigour, and there was a muted but still emphatic arrogance about his manner which was not entirely off-set by the casual informality of his greeting. His eyes were a pleasant blue but, on inspection, coldly inquisitive, and his lips were thin and rather mean. He was evidently self-possessed, sure of his ground, at perfect ease among strangers, and, so Davis thought as he shook hands, shrewdly analytic.

"Thank you all for coming at such short notice," Hoffman said, in an accent considerably and audibly softened by a long acquaintance with European manners.

"Let's have a drink, shall we?"

He led the way into an adjoining, dimly-lit bar. A few of the tables were still occupied but they found an empty one in a

20

quiet corner and Hoffman ordered drinks: the waiter came and went.

"First, let me get your names straight," the American began, looking at them over his glass. The mercenaries, all of them well aware that Hoffman probably already knew them by photographic means or even by sight, went through the ritual of formal introductions. "Right," he continued, "now I'll tell you something about myself — as much, anyway, as you need to know — and then, if that's all right, we'll proceed to the project". He paused momentarily. "I guess you don't mind me talking in here?"

"No," Christie confirmed. "We don't mind at all —— here — anywhere."

Hoffman smiled appreciatively.

"Good. Well, you know my name, but you don't know that I'm on the board of a large American banking concern based in Miami, Florida. It's simply called the American Bank —". He felt in his top pocket and produced a number of small, neatly, and expensively, printed business cards, flicking them across the table. The cards carried the appropriate information. "It's important that we trust one another", Hoffman explained. "From the start."

Christie turned the card over, face down on the table, but said nothing.

Having got the names straight with the faces, the slim, well-dressed American began to tell a story that gripped the three Englishmen's attention so tightly that when supper was announced the three men were reluctant to go and eat for fear of losing the thread of the story.

"My bank is a reasonably substantial concern, even by American standards," continued Hoffman after they'd been seated in the coffee bar and had all ordered a light meal. "And there are branches of the bank now in most major cities — Sydney, New York, London, Beirut, Zurich, and so on. Only one of those branches, however, concerns us at the moment." He paused again, emptied his glass and looked around for the waiter. Tippett was also momentarily distracted by the sight of a slim, long-legged girl in a tight blue, backless gown slit to the waist who had glanced discreetly in their direction as she crossed the room. The mercenary watched her disappear, noticing how the material of the gown cleaved to her shape, revealing its geography.

Reluctantly he returned his attention to Hoffman's monologue, just as the American revealed, without causing any surprise, that Beirut was the branch in question. He proceeded, at some length, to tell them why, explaining that a certain amount of background information might be useful to them if they accepted the contract. He began by pointing out that Beirut is, and always has been, the commercial clearing house of the Middle East. Ideally situated on the shores of the Mediterranean it plays host to a nation of traders, and since it is also on the main overland route to Arabia its commercial advantages are obvious. Hoffman's American Bank, like many others of its kind, established a branch there almost as a matter of course. There was no question, however, of them moving into new premises so they bought an old, slightly delapidated but still elegant mansion house on the fringe of what was then the banking sector, just north of the town's centre. It took almost a year to renovate, rebuild and adapt the building to its new purpose, during which time the bank imported and installed all the latest American technological equipment, including advanced computers and a highly sophisticated telecommunications system. The bank also ordered specially-designed and purpose built strong-room doors and vaults. That, at least, Hoffman emphasized, made it unique among its competitors — a privilege preserved, to some extent, by the precautionary secrecy surrounding the importation and fitting of the doors.

All this, of course, added considerably to the already enormous capital investment. But the rewards were staggering — so much so that, after only five lucrative years of trading, the directors were ready to consider opening a second, smaller branch in the City. Then, with the suddenness of a summer storm, came the first signs of political trouble.

Hoffman, at this point, felt it would be equally valuable to explain some of the background to the Civil War which had already reduced much of the picturesque city to rubble. He told them that, despite the presence of innumerable political and religious factions in the country — principally the Moslem Arabs and the Christian Arabs, or Phalangists — there had traditionally been less internal strife in the Lebanon than in most Middle East States. The third and fourth Arab wars against the Israelis, however, changed all that by displacing hundreds of thousands of Palestinian Arabs who fled into Jordan, Egypt, Syria and the Lebanon. From these countries, having established a political movement at first called Al Fatah, they began to wage a periodic guerrilla war against the Zionist State, which responded in turn, to outrages like the massacre at Lod airport, with Commando raids deep inside the Palestinian strongholds, bombing and machine-gunning the great camps of cardboard and corrugated iron which housed the refugees. The war merely escalated. Soon the Israelis were turning their attentions towards the host countries' own establishments. In 1968 an Israeli commando raid on Khaldi Airport, Beirut, destroyed a number of civil aircraft. The action was condemned by Beirut's Moslem Arabs, who were naturally sympathetic to the Palestinian cause; but it was condoned, even applauded, by the Christian Arabs, thus driving a thick wedge between the two communities. It was only a matter of time before these deep divisions, in the context of a combustible political situation throughout the entire Middle East, flared into open civil war.

Not surprisingly, however, the bank, during all this time, simply kept on trading. The war, as wars often do, proved to be good for business. By now well-established, with a good international reputation, it attracted Beirut's wealthy families who began to rent safety deposit boxes by the dozen in which to store away their jewelry and their money, keeping both safe from the looters who swarmed, day and night, over the city.

"It's strange," Hoffman reflected, "how life goes on even in the most extreme circumstances. Beirut was, quite literally, being gutted. Buildings burnt, were blown away, machine gun fire raked the streets, armed civilians, belonging to one camp or the other, one religion or another, were patrolling freely, stopping cars, murdering, mutilating, torturing, accepting no explanations. But it wasn't just the bank which continued to function. It was the people. Oh, yes, hundreds left. But thousands stayed, even the rich. Perhaps they thought, living on the hillsides, that the war would never touch them. At night, no doubt, they watched the flames spurting below, and smelt the gasoline. They observed with interest or horror their tranquil city being consumed by fire. But then neighbours and friends started to die. The war reached their villas. Still they stayed on, going down the hill to find an enterprisingly open shop or deposit another set of jewels at the bank. They adapted. They endured, I suppose, as people do." He shook his head at the thought. "I visited the bank once or twice. It wasn't pleasant. The second time I was there they assassinated the American Ambassador."

Davis, interested despite a certain familiarity with Middle East politics (like most mercenaries he was well versed in political geography), lit another cigarette, coughed and indicated his empty glass.

"Is that when the Embassy packed it in?" he wondered.

"Yes," the American confirmed. "I'll get you another."

They paused to allow the waiter time to bring a fresh round of drinks. In the civility of the Hilton's lower bar, talking of civil war seemed incongruous. On the other hand it always started like this, as if an invisible thread stretched from hotel lobby to Africa or Beirut, along which first their thoughts and then they themselves would travel.

Davis looked up, and smiled ironically as a group of Arabs left their table and walked past theirs, talking volubly.

"Thanks," he said, lifting his glass.

"At that time," continued Hoffman, taking up the thread, "the banking sector seemed pretty secure in any case. It was very definitely in Christian-held territory. With the Embassy

24

gone, naturally people started to talk seriously of closing down and leaving, but you'll understand that wasn't an easy decision to make. Compared to moving a bank, an Embassy is like pitching a tent. So we hung on. We kept hearing reports that the PLO forces were getting closer, but then the reports would be denied, you know how it is, though we did know that by that time the Russians were supplying a lot of hardware. Then, suddenly, nothing. A lull. No more reports of any enchroachments. Only sporadic fighting. Nothing!"

Hoffman shrugged his shoulders — a casual gesture immediately contradicted by a narrowing of his cold, blue eyes.

"That was three weeks ago. The bank, of course, kept trading, keeping a weather eye out but no more than that. Some kind of normality returned." He paused again, heightening the effect of his next statement. "Three days ago the entire banking sector, intact, fell to the PLO"

Davis hadn't known.

"How?"

Hoffman's smile was thin and humourless.

"They went down into the sewers. The Christian's hadn't checked. That was that."

"The fortunes of war," Tippett said, thinking of the money, but when his eyes met Hoffman's they found agreement.

"Right. In just two days they've opened no less than nine principal banks including the largest one in the whole Middle East, the British Bank. Out of that one alone they took an estimated two hundred million dollars. Enough to buy Israel back at Hollywood real estate prices."

It wasn't a joke.

"What's happened to your bank?" Christie wanted to know.

"My bank is the only one that remains, up until tonight at least, still unopened. There's a good reason for that; and the reason weighs approximately nine tons — the vault door. Oh, they've tried to blow it, apparently killing one of their men in the process. But they've only succeeded in tripping all the devices, including the tungsten bars."

25

"Why haven't they gone round the door and through the wall instead?" asked Tippett bluntly.

"Precisely what they did in the British Bank." Hoffman's response was nearly smug. "They can't do that with our vault, it's almost as strong as the door itself. I told you we were careful."

Tippett acknowledged the fact thoughtfully. Even with his experience a door like that would cause one or two problems — unless, of course, the earlier attempts had left just the thinnest of cracks. He would need to see a few photographs to be sure, and he doubted whether anyone could now procure them.

Davis, too, had been silent for a while. There was nevertheless something he wanted to know very much.

"How do you know all this."

"From Danny Chamoun," was the prompt and totally unexpected reply.

"Chamoun?" Davis's voice betrayed his surprise. Danny Chamoun was the leader of the Christians in Beirut, and a figure of considerable stature. Davis had heard a great deal about him, much of it, without a doubt, apocryphal and untrue, but all of it sufficiently impressive to suggest something of the quality and charisma of the man. Perhaps unwillingly, Davis experienced a vague and new sense of respect.

"How well do you know Chamoun?" he probed.

"I've met him. Twice, three times."

"Recently?"

"Yes. And we keep in contact, of course."

Davis had to admire the American's skill as a manipulator of interest, as well as the subtle way in which he continually authenticated his own position. He was prepared to believe that only perversity kept his suspicions alive.

"Needless to say, Chamoun is not my only source of information regarding the bank, so when I tell you that I expect the vault to remain intact for two, maybe three weeks more, you will have to accept that this estimation is based on fairly comprehensive and reliable intelligence reports. We are also, of course, taking into account the opinion of the vault and door manufacturers. Anyway, it is an assumption we are obliged to treat as a fact. Please bear it in mind." He stopped and looked across at them quickly. "Now, there is, as you would expect, a large safety deposit section in the vault, and in that section there are six boxes of particular interest to us. Why they are of interest is naturally no concern of yours — but getting them out could be."

Hoffman, very slightly, lowered the tone of his voice.

"The deal I'm putting to you all is this. We want those boxes. We're prepared to hire a small team of specialists, probably six men including yourselves, to work in coordination with the Christian forces. Chamoun has already prepared and briefed a group of his own men and there won't be any difficulty on the ground once you're there. I'm afraid you'll have to take my word for that."

Christie, leaning forward suddenly, interrupted him sharply, his hands flat on the table.

"How much are you paying, Mr Hoffman?"

"We are prepared to pay a reasonable — but not extravagant — sum up front . . . and offer you a bonus."

"What's that?"

"The bonus would be exactly half the remaining monies in the vault strongboxes. A considerable sum. Naturally we keep, as far as possible, a record of all transactions at the bank and, believe me, we have a fair idea of the amount you're likely to find. Only a fair idea though. The real amount is incalculable."

"You wouldn't hazard a guess?" Tippett wondered.

Hoffman shook his head apologetically. "No, I wouldn't. I don't want to be responsible for exaggerated expectations. This is a gamble for all of us, Mr Tippett."

"You mean a lot of the boxes or their contents might have been removed during the time the bank was taken, or even before?" queried Christie.

"Unlikely. In the first place no-one was authorized to take such action, and in the second place everything happened too quickly and unexpectedly. In any case I've promised Chamoun, for his part, the other half of the money. If he's not satisfied, well . . ." Hoffman opened out his palms, and smiled.

"Look," Davis said, "if he's not satisfied, where does that leave us? He's not likely to let us walk away with half of not very much."

"You're right to be cautious," the American agreed seriously. "But Chamoun has got too much to lose to play games with you. I'm afraid I can't let you in on the politics. You'll just have to believe that the bank has every reason to expect Chamoun's co-operation and good faith. He's a man of his word."

Davis checked to see if Hoffman actually believed it, but he could detect nothing from the other man's expression. Hoffman might be lying or he might not, though for some reason, on this occasion, he was inclined to believe him. He could already sense that the other two did probably because, whatever the risks, the rewards sounded commensurate. He waited for one of them to continue questioning Hoffman's preparations, since it seemed to him that the American had a lot more explaining to do before they could begin to make even a provisional decision. But neither of them spoke.

"How much are you offering up front for a start?" he asked after a moment, returning to an earlier point and determined to extract some form of commitment.

"Two thousand pounds per man," Hoffman replied. "Half when we agree. Half later."

"That's not enough."

"For two weeks work? In all conscience, and in view of the expected returns, I think it's a reasonable payment. But I think we should talk about this again tomorrow evening. We have a great deal more to discuss, as I'm sure you must appreciate. All I require from you now is some indication of your interest."

"We're very interested," Christie spoke for them. "We'll want to know more, but for the moment everything sounds fine."

"Good. We'll meet again, here, tomorrow night at eight, but this time I think we'll find a more private room. I want you to meet someone from the vault manufacturers, and you will have to convince him, and me that you are capable of getting through the door and into the vault itself. I trust that's not a disagreeable condition? In the meantime, let me remind you that time is very short. You will have to make a final decision tomorrow whatever happens, and you should therefore anticipate leaving the country no more than three or four days after that. I hope that's clear. Now, I expect you would like to go away and discuss the proposition. Frankly, I would be astonished if you declined it, but I'm sure there are others who would not?" Hoffman stood up. "Before you go, let me give you these." He handed across three bulky brown envelopes. "Your expenses. Tomorrow at eight, then."

They followed him through into the foyer but he was already gone. Outside, the rain had slackened to a thin, permeating drizzle, and only Tippett felt like talking as they walked quickly towards the car. He wanted to talk about the girl in the slit skirt. Neither Davis nor Christie had noticed her. Neither had the slightest bit of interest in Tippett's lurid fantasies, elaborated at length and in considerable detail on the journey back. All Davis could think of was that in a few days time he would no longer be in England, that he had already begun the journey that would take him, once again, to war.

3

The name of the girl in the slit skirt was Susan, or Susie, Litworth. She was the eldest daughter of a farmer in Gloucestershire, but had moved to London when she was seventeen to avoid marrying another farmer's son. For two years she had earned a meagre living as a temporary typist in various offices, most of them around Campden Town and Wandsworth. She had hated it so much, had felt so lonely and desperate, that she had nearly returned to the farmhouse and a conveniently dull marriage. Then, one night outside a cinema, a man, a complete stranger, had offered her money to sleep with him, since he too was away from home and lonely. Humiliated and shocked she had run away. A year later, she had finally stopped running away, although she would still not contemplate doing business outside a cinema, like a prostitute.

For Susie worked the big London hotels now, exclusively. She was paid very well and everything was equally well organised, very much on a closed shop principal. Tonight she had been told to meet an American called Martin Hoffman, and had looked for him, first in the foyer and then the bars of the Hilton. When, finally, he had emerged, she had greeted him with a quick, affectionate kiss and linked her arm through his. She was rather surprised when Hoffman guided her out-side, into the rain (she had not been told about his flat) but she was equally relieved that he was American and not Arab.

Hoffman hardly noticed how young she was — he had almost forgotten the arrangement — and he was certainly in no mood for conversation as he drove back, fast, to Knightsbridge. But Susie was not in the least unnerved by his silence. There was no particular reason for them to talk. She had nothing particular to say to him. So she merely set back in the keep leather seat, enjoying its temporary comfort, and kept her hands primly together on her lap.

Once inside the flat, Hoffman almost changed his mind. He felt no real sexual interest in the girl. She did not interest or stimulate him, and there were, as usual, things he had to do.

He switched on the main light in the living room, hung his coat behind the door, and poured a single whisky. Then he walked over to the study, still carrying his attache case, holding the half-full glass in his other hand. He paused in the doorway.

"Take your coat off," he said, looking at her for the first time under the light with indifferent curiosity. "Sit down and wait."

He went into the study and closed the door. She could hear him dialling, one number after another, cursing as he stopped, began again, dialling indefinitely. She could even hear his voice — clipped, firm, impatient — but not the words.

She removed her coat and combed out her long, damp hair before the mirror. She sat down, away from the door, near the window, looking out briefly at the dark, wet sky, noticing a few yellow lights in other windows.

The door opened. Hoffman checked to see where she was in the room, regarding her silently, coldly. He went back inside, closing the door, and this time she couldn't hear him dialling or even his voice. She looked at the nearly empty bookshelves against the wall, at the clean, white surfaces of the room, harsh and cold under the naked light, at the large, still glove in the corner. She lit a cigarette.

After a while, Hoffman came back into the room, a bleak smile on his face, which wasn't for her. She saw how tired he was. There were small, wrinkled sacks of darker flesh under his eyes, a deep line running down each brown cheek. He took his jacket off and threw it over the back of a chair. He was

31

carrying no loose change, she saw, because it would have fallen out of his pockets then.

"Okay," he said. "Get up."

He watched her undress in silence, making no movement towards the bedroom and with apparent disinterest. He made no attempt to touch her, and she detected neither anticipation nor anger in the eyes that watched her face. She was not disappointed. She felt that he must share the deliberate but careful contempt she felt towards her own body. Soon it was naked.

"Are you ready?" Hoffman said.

She nodded her head and, on impulse, lowered her eyes obediently. Suddenly she had no desire to talk, to utter a word. She hoped he would not demand it of her, prompt her in any way. If, she thought, there could be total silence. No voices, no passion, no plastic involvement, just the performance.

Hoffman continued to look at the girl's naked form coldly. She waited. She felt the small hard goose pimples, like a rash, spreading down her arms, her back. Hoffman walked back into the other room and told her to get dressed — he'd changed his mind.

Before going to bed that night, Davis put a call through to a number in Norwich. It was two thirty in the morning. He let the number ring for a long time, lighting another cigarette with his free hand.

Eventually someone picked up the telephone at the other end.

"Who's that?"

"For God's sake. It's fucking three in the morning, Tom".

"Yes, I know, I'm sorry"

"I'm still half asleep" the distant voice complained.

Davis, too tired himself to make any more token apologies, snapped down the phone:

"This is important, Bill. Are you listening?"

The complaint died away to a sour, importunate grumble.

"If it's that important. . . ."

Davis could suddenly picture the other and older man, no doubt dressed in striped and faded pyjamas, leaning unsteadily against the telephone table, his mind foggy with alcohol as it always was.

"It is," he insisted curtly. "Look, I want you to do something for me. Do you still have that contact in the American embassy?"

"Yes"

"Could you get him to run a check, personal wise. I'll give you the details in a second. What is very important is that I get this information by tomorrow. Can you deliver that quick?"

There was a pause at the other end of the line as the elderly reporter tried to marshal his thoughts.

"All right — anything you say."

"Thanks," Davis said, his tone softening in conciliation. "His name is Hoffman — on the board of an American banking corporation, called The American Bank — have you got all that, this bank is based in Miami."

The voice at the other end murmured its assent.

"By tomorrow then." He put the phone down without waiting for any other response. Davis, although tired physically, knew that sleep would elude him for a while yet. His Great Dane came and leant against him and stuck a huge, wet, black nose into his hand.

"Christ, I haven't fed you tonight." The man, followed by the two wagging tails, went into the kitchen and spooned out a Chinese takeaway into the two dogs' bowls. It was another hour before he slipped gratefully into his bed, but not before he'd smoked another five Silk Cut cigarettes and had examined the contents of Hoffman's envelope.

The next evening Hoffman introduced the three mercenaries to the safe expert from the vault door manufacturers, a small, sandy-haired American called Will Lindquist who had flown over that morning from Paris to meet with them. Lindquist appeared, to Davis at least, nervous and ill at ease. He fiddled constantly with his wedding ring and as he talked, drawing out each word with a faint suggestion of impediment, he kept looking towards Hoffman, as if for reassurence. But Hoffman, as collected and impeccable as the night before, remained detached, looking on from his seat under the window and then, after a while, requesting a quiet word with Christie.

As the two men disappeared Davis reflected on his sense of surprise at Christie's willingness to join the expedition in the first place. Neither he nor Tippett had expected the recruiter and arms dealer to do any more than orchestrate from behind the scenes. But Christie stated his intention flatly: he had every intention of going to Beirut, and they were certainly in no position to quarrel with the decision. In private, they had naturally speculated both on the man's motives and on his actual capacities as a soldier. As far as they knew Christie, despite his vast web of contacts, had never gone to war as a mercenary, and they still knew little about his time with the British army, though Christie had mentioned his proficiency with fire arms.

The most likely explanation for his decision was, clearly, the promise of instant riches. He probably distrusted Davis and Tippett as much as they mistrusted him, and was therefore anxious to participate in the actual raid and the distribution of the spoils. But Davis still felt vaguely uneasy in the face of Hoffman's desires to survive. And yet there are degrees of trust and dependence, and in an operation of this kind, involving a small team of men, the presence of one man like Christie could be compromising and dangerous. In Davis's eyes that was an important consideration, especially now, at the beginning. But without Tippett's active support there was little chance of even publicly questioning Christie's participation. And as he watched him now across the room, deep in conversation with the American, his rat-like features pinched in an expression of pensive contemplation, he acknowledged silently that there was a great deal he would have to accept, unwillingly, as the days went on. He could only assume that the prize was worth the compromises and doubts, the calculated but open-ended risks so familiar to the mercenary but not the soldier.

He turned his attentions to the nearer, less intimate conversation between Tippett and Lindquist. The American had recovered, it seemed, much of his lost composure. It was clear that he felt increasingly comfortable as he began to discuss technical matters with the British explosives expert, and already the table between them was thick with, to Davis, inexplicably abstract folios illustrating the construction and design of the massive vault door. Tippett examined certain of the major features and didn't disguise the fact that the door presented a formidable challenge, especially if it remained structurally undamaged.

Lindquist explained what he assumed had occurred during the previous attempts to breach the four-feet thick metal and then, surprisingly, produced a series of twenty-by-twenty black and white prints showing its state four days previously. Tippett studied the photographs carefully and without comment. Superficially the door appeared very badly damaged; twisted shards of discoloured metal punctured its surface, like strips of damp, curling wallpaper. But the mess was just that — purely superficial. On closer examination, as Lindquist had forecast, it remained in perfect shape, discouragingly so.

Under the light of an Anglepoise lamp Tippett went over each large photograph again and again, hoping to see evidence of even a minute but deep-enough fracture. At last he detected something, possibly a fissure, down in the left hand corner and partially disguised by a dark, cordite stain.

He examined the place in each photograph with the use of Lindquist's magnifying glass, calculating as he did so the volume of the strong room itself and the quantity of explosives necessary to complete the job. In all probability, he thought, he could make do with no more than two pints of nitroglycerine — in which case, why had the Palestinians given up? The fracture would be very obvious to anyone inspecting the door with their fingers. It seemed absurd that they had given up at the point of success.

35

He expressed his surprise to the American, who simply shrugged.

"It doesn't surprise me," he said. "Anomalies like that are common in war. It just appears they don't possess the expertise, at least for the moment. Maybe they're superstitious after one of them died trying to open it. Who knows? Now they're just sitting tight. But I couldn't say for how long."

Hoffman joined them at the table and caught Tippett's eye.

"All I want to know is whether *you* can guarantee to complete the job, once we get you there," he said coldly. "Well?"

Tippett paused, then smiled.

"No question. There's a small crack down there," He indicated it with a ringed finger. "That's all I needed."

"I heard about the Berlin job — and the bank at Marseilles," Lindquist interrupted suddenly. "Very impressive and professional." He seemed genuinely pleased to be able to flatter the mercenary.

Tippett, suppressing a gesture of surprise, was less pleased that a complete stranger appeared in full possession of his private history.

He looked at Hoffman. Hoffman's expression acknowledged a similar privilege, and he might have repaid Lindquist's compliment. It was all very impressive and professional.

Tippett didn't allow himself to dwell on the matter.

"I'll need two pints of grease," he informed Lindquist, noticing how, in Hoffman's presence, the man had once again started to play with his wedding ring.

"Can you prepare it yourself?" the American asked.

The mercenary nodded. "If you supply the materials."

He enumerated them slowly, so that Lindquist could jot down the prescription for acids in his notebook.

"And an ice-making machine," he added. "Oh, and a portable air-extraction unit — for the sake of my lungs."

Lindquist put them down in small, neat print.

"How long will it take you?" he wondered.

"Between two and three days."

"Good," Hoffman said. "It would be convenient," he went on "if we flew all the materials to Cyprus. We have a safe house there. I'll arrange for the transportation and see that everything arrives the day after tomorrow. Now, is there anything else you want to ask Will here? No?"

He glanced across at Lindquist.

"Then I think this would be a suitable moment for you to step out, Will, if you don't mind. Okay?"

Lindquist stood up, patently happy to be excused. He shook hands with Tippett.

"Good luck," he said.

"Thanks. I hope we don't need it."

Hoffman waited until the door had closed.

"Can I take it that nothing you have heard so far has caused you to reconsider your original interest?" He looked at each of them in turn, impassively.

"You can take it we're still interested," Davis said.

"But?"

"But we want two extras. The first is an increase in manpower, from six to nine men. The second is more money up front. Frankly, we're not happy to go out for just a few hundred pounds, hard cash."

He looked at the others for confirmation. They had already argued over the new conditions and both Tippett and Christie had expressed a strong desire to avoid antagonizing Hoffman and jeopardizing the operation. But Davis had insisted that six men left them too short of cover. Moreover, that afternoon, his contact had reported back that Hoffman's association with the American Bank of Miami was simply in an advisory capacity, a somewhat more peripheral rôle than the American himself had suggested. Whilst that information alone was hardly enough to incriminate him it was nevertheless significant enough to justify a certain caution.

Under sustained pressure the others had finally conceded the point though now, as Davis glanced across towards them, they did no more than nod in perfunctory agreement.

But it was enough to cause Hoffman to walk back to the window, apparently deep in thought. For a few moments they could see his reflection in the dark glass. Then he came back.

"I'll agree to the second," he said eventually, "but not the first." He rested his arms against the back of a chair. "In this context, nine men would amount to a small army. Moving them around would cause problems; and I suspect you might have difficulty recruiting them at such short notice. If you move at all, you move in two or three days time. I thought that was understood?"

"Recruitment's no problem," Davis argued stubbornly. "I presume you have no objection to our arranging that?"

Hoffman shook his head, suppressing a smile.

"None at all. That's your business. I just require a list of names and perhaps a little information about each man. Apart from anything else, I shall need bank account numbers, unless you want to be paid differently? *But*, I'm afraid, I only want six names and six numbers, not nine."

Davis failed to respond.

"How much more cash are we talking about?" Tippett butted in.

Hoffman laced his fingers together carefully, and paused.

"I intend to double the original fee. The usual terms. Half before you leave, half on your return. I trust that's satisfactory?"

"Look!" Christie said, clearly anxious to rescue the situation. "We don't want to pull out, especially if the money's right, so perhaps . . ."

"I'll agree to seven," Hoffman interrupted sharply. "No more. Take it or leave it."

Christie and Tippett, won over as Davis knew even before the start of the meeting, waited for him to agree. He did so with a small, reluctant gesture, that might have seemed ambiguous, and lit another cigarette. Hoffman immediately adopted a milder, more conciliatory tone.

"That's excellent! If I can have the names by tomorrow, if possible . . ."

He produced a further two brown envelopes, giving the first to Christie.

"Here's fifteen hundred to be shared out among the new recruits."

The second he handed to Tippett.

"I expect you'll need to buy some equipment. That should be more than sufficient to cover everything. Naturally you don't have to worry about essentials. At the right time you will be issued with suitable weapons, and you can leave the transportation to us." He continued to Tippett directly. "As the explosives will doubtless take some time to prepare, I think it would be better if you were to leave England first. I'm prepared to charter a freight plane to transport your materials to Cyprus and I suggest you travel with it. I'll arrange for it to stop at Gatwick airport the day after tomorrow. Please be ready to join it there. There shouldn't be any problems with Customs. You are one of my mechanics — and I have the appropriate papers in my bag. You do, of course, possess a valid passport?"

"Yes," Tippett said. "No problem."

Hoffman smiled. "I trust not."

"What about the rest of us?" Davis asked.

"If the situation in Beirut remains stable, and unless I hear to the contrary, you will leave for Cyprus, in two parties, the day after Mr Tippett's departure; in other words, on the fourteenth of this month. You will travel on regular flights, landing at Larnaka airport, and from there you will make your way to separate hotels in the town. Your plane tickets, and the names of the hotels, will be supplied tomorrow afternoon or evening, in exchange for a list of names. At that time, too, you will be paid the first half of your fee. Or, if you prefer, I will arrange to have two thousand pounds transferred straight into your accounts. You will be able to check that the transaction has been accomplished from Cyprus, otherwise you will be perfectly at liberty to abort the assignment then and there.

"But let us assume you decide to go ahead. In that case you will be accountable to my assistant, Robert Sneiger, who will

39

be making contact with you as soon as you have settled into your hotels. He will be responsible for briefing you on the lay-out of the bank, and anything else you need to know about the operation inside Beirut. Then, I think one day later, you will be taken by boat across to the Lebanon, accompanied by Sneiger, where you will make contact with a group of Phalangists, and proceed in due course to your destination."

"What transport are we going in with?" asked Davis, practical as ever.

"The Phalangists will provide you with an armoured vehicle of some kind, if that's any use to you. Otherwise I suggest you give me some idea of your requirements and they will be conveyed. Remember, you will be leaving the bank with a number of heavy boxes, a great deal of money, presumably in bulky sacks, and seven men."

But Davis had already decided what they would need.

"I'd prefer to modify either a long wheel-base Landrover or a small truck," he said. "And I'd want plenty of materials, even if it's scrap metal, and a few basic cutting and welding tools."

"I'll tell them to have everything ready."

Hoffman didn't need to make notes. He stood up, turned away and went over to a small table containing a number of bottles and glasses.

"Bourbon okay with you?"

"If that's all you've got . . ."

He returned with the glasses and sat down, handing them around.

"What happens when we've done the job?" Tippett wondered, swilling the dark beverage around the clear glass in his hand. "How long will we have, and how do we get out?"

"As to the first question, I've no idea," Hoffman said. "Sneiger will be able to give you more details about the actual operation, as I've already said. But upon completion you will drive north, with an escort for at least part of the journey, towards Tripoli . . ."

Before he could go on, Davis said curtly,

40

"Show us."

Hoffman fetched his large marked map of the Middle East and spread it out on the floor between them. He indicated where they would land after the proposed crossing from Larnaka — an uninhabited spot well to the north of Beirut — then followed the coastal road into the city with his index finger. The same road would take them back out again.

"Again you will divide into two parties," he said. "A boat will be waiting here, just to the north of the town of Jelail. Sneiger will know the exact location. But the second group will continue along the road to Tripoli, and catch a regular flight back to London." Hoffman, pausing, stroked his hair back with his free hand. "The safety deposit boxes will, of course, travel with the party on the boat. We do not anticipate your encountering any problems with Israeli patrol boats in the area, and in any case Sneiger will know how to deal with such a contingency. In short, you will be chauffeured there and back, with little to worry you except the actual raid on the bank. I'm buying your expertise. There's nothing more to it than that."

Davis said grudgingly,

"That seems clear enough," and looked at the narrow, purple strip of land on the map that now seemed disproportionately significant, hedged in as it was by its greater Arab neighbours.

"Where am I making the grease?" Tippett interjected.

"There's a safe house in Cyprus. You will be met at the airport and taken there."

"And how will we recognise your boxes?"

"You won't!" Hoffman was almost sharp. "That's Sneiger's responsibility. The boxes are nothing to do with you. I trust that's understood?"

"Of course," Christie said placatingly.

Hoffman folded up the map, replacing it fastidiously.

"Now," he said, "I think we have something to celebrate. In roughly three weeks time you will all be very rich men. We

41

should drink to that." **And he** smiled at them pleasantly, and watched them over the top of his glass.

"Cheers!" Tippett said, happily.

Hoffman got to his feet again, leaving the glasses empty.

"If there's nothing more to discuss . . .? Good, I think we can say goodbye for the moment. I assume I shall see one of you tomorrow, so if anything else should occur to you . . ." he left the implication in the air.

"I'll be in touch," Christie confirmed, offering his hand.

"I'm sure," Hoffman said.

Makmoud was, as usual, tinkering about with the engine of his car. It was an old rusted American car — a Ford Ranchero — the body stained in several places with rust but the engine ran as beautifully and smoothly as the day Henry Ford built it, and Makmoud was immensely, inordinately proud of it. He was not concerned with the rust. He had hardly touched the body-work since the day he had stolen the car, three months ago, because people would have taken more notice of a shiny, polished, expensive-looking vehicle. They might have mistaken him for a rich Lebanese, like the car's previous owner, and one fine day, when he started the engine, both he and his beloved machine would simply have disappeared, incinerated in the blinking of an eye.

After all, that *was* what had happened to the previous owner (Makmoud had planted the bomb himself), only on that occasion Makmoud had experimented with a very small charge designed to kill or maim the driver but leave the car largely undamaged. As it was, there was now a hole, underneath, covered by a strip of carpet, and Makmoud had had to replace the shattered windscreen. But his plan had succeeded brilliantly. His experience with planting explosives had served him well. He patted the discoloured dark grey body of the car affectionately.

Makmoud looked like a Cypriot (people always told him that) with his long, curly, jet-black hair and olive-coloured

42

skin, his habit of gesturing theatrically with his hands as he spoke, but he was actually Lebanese. Certainly he had been sent to Cyprus in 1954, to study, when he was fourteen years of age, and had stayed long enough to join EOKA, the guerrilla force led by his hero, General Grivas. A young and inexperienced volunteer, Makmoud had nevertheless been responsible for destroying, virtually single-handed, a British transport plane at Nicosia airport. He was then sixteen years of age. Grivas himself had congratulated him and personally awarded a small medal, made out of tin, which Makmoud still kept hidden away in a drawer, though it had tarnished and there were no words on it.

Next came the 1967 war against the Israelis. (There was, in Makmoud's experience, always a war.) He had been wounded and left for dead by his friends in the great retreat across to the West Bank in Jordan. He was taken prisoner of war. To his great surprise the Zionists did not dismember him, or shoot him, merely dressed his wounds and fed him. He returned home with a changed point of view, and even the Yom Kippur war of 1973 failed to alter his new allegiance. So, when the Palestinians started to cause trouble in his own country, claiming that every Arab had a duty to bring the State of Israel to an end, he naturally joined with Danny Chamoun who led the Phalangists, and joined the Civil War. Now he had a good reputation as a street fighter and nobody worried about his American car, as long as it looked rusty.

Makmoud wiped his blackened hands on an old cloth and stood up straight, his head to one side, listening. The explosion must have happened a few miles away, perhaps in the banking sector now in the hands of the armed elements of the PLO. He spat copiously and threw the cloth away, looking up at the clear blue sky for the column of smoke. He could see nothing — it might have been a small car bomb, the noise carrying on the still air — except the rough and jagged skyline where mortars and bombs and fires had dismantled the tops of the tall buildings and blackened the walls.

It brought a quickening to his pulses everytime he surveyed

the damage. He was not at all concerned that Beirut had once been beautiful, an elegant city. Then it had always been full of tourists and foreigners and the ostentatiously rich, looking down from their verandas and palaces. Now, a city at war, everything had changed for the better. For Makmoud the city had come to life. You could feel its energy everywhere on the streets and running through the blood. You could hear it in the rattle of machine gun fire, smell it on the air, chemical and acrid. Excitement and terror together. From the very earliest years, as a wild, wilful and adventurous child, Makmoud had sought excitement and terror. But whereas once he had climbed trees and thieved, now he killed, for a cause. His life had a great and consuming purpose. He was one and happy.

He walked away from the car, down the quiet street of poor, dilapidated dwellings, avoiding the rubble and the uncollected human refuse. At the end of the street he could see part of the crude barricade, but no sign of a soldier. Only a few cars ever used this street now, although a few nights previously an unknown sniper had picked off one of the guards with a single shot. The dead man had been one of Makmoud's oldest friends. Makmoud had buried him with his own hands in the wasteland behind the houses, and then he had crossed to another sector and waited for a car. He let four cars pass. The fifth car was a Mercedes. Makmoud shattered its windows with machine gun fire as it drove past him, watched it swerve suddenly and roll to a stop, on the other side of the road, about one hundred yards from where he was standing. He waited for a few moments but no-one opened the door. Then he had slipped away into the shadows, his friend avenged.

From the doorway of one of the small, shuttered houses a man gestured him over. The man had a rifle, a Russian Kalashnikov, cradled in his arms, and a scarf wrapped around his head. Makmoud nodded to him as he entered the house. Inside it was hot and dark. He opened a door and went down a flight of stone steps into the cellar. A single electric light bulb illuminated the bare, damp, cheerless room, furnished with a number of wooden chairs, a card table and, against the wall, a metal rack full of rifles. Three of the chairs were already occupied. Makmoud sat down.

The man sitting behind the card table facing him handed across two brightly coloured photographs. Makmoud studied the faces in the photographs.

"The first man's name is Michael Tippett," the man behind the desk said at last. "The one with dark hair and the scar. An explosives expert from England. You will meet him in Cyprus, at Larnaka airport, in two days, take him to the house and help him make explosives." He paused. To Makmoud the silence seemed very oppressive. "The other man is Tom Davis, also English, who fixes engines, like you. Can you find him a truck or a Landrover?"

Makmoud said, yes, he could find either.

"Good. By tomorrow, then."

Makmoud stood up.

"Sit down, Makmoud!" The man made an impatient gesture with his right hand.

"I will tell you that these men are coming here to break the American Bank. You know the American Bank? Good. You will be with them all the time. There will be others, of course, but you will be in charge, unofficially. There will be six English mercenaries. You will naturally have to be careful when you deal with them. But . . . if you deal with them properly there may be a reward."

Makmoud's dark eyes glinted.

"A medal — just like your other one."

The olive-coloured face opened suddenly in a delighted grin.

"You can go now," the man said, leaning back against his chair.

"Yes." Makmoud stood up again. "Thank you, Danny."

Chamoun heard his footsteps on the stone steps.

"Fucking English mercenaries," he said bitterly. "Fuck them."

4

After some discussion the three principals finally agreed on a list of twelve possible names for the four remaining positions on the team. Contacting the men involved — which would entail a few long-distance phone calls and a visit to the British army barracks at Aldershot — was left to Christie and Davis. Tippett's job was to buy the radios, webbing harnesses, medical kits and anything else which might be useful and could be easily carried.

"Like a good book to read on the plane," he joked, before leaving for London in the Scimitar.

Davis's first calls, were local, to a small transport yard in Sandhurst, a village close to Camberley and a certain noted military establishment. On the way he dropped the two dogs off at the local kennels, where they were familiar inmates. Mrs Wodehouse, fat and kind and fussy, greeted them effusively in her cluttered office.

"Hello, my darlings! Have we come for a holiday then?"

Davis found her matronly habits tolerably amusing, and laughed. She stood up.

"You're away again, then, Mr Davis?" she said, with a hint of reproach.

"For about a month."

She regarded him through her thick pebble glasses.

"Somewhere nice?"

"Scotland."

"I see!" Mrs Wodehouse's tone was cold with contempt:

clearly a trip to Scotland was no excuse for abandoning two poor, dependent animals.

Davis excused himself.

"Well, Mr Davis, I do hope you have a nice trip," Mrs Wodehouse concluded, with a thin smile.

"Thank you. I'll try to bring you back something."

She nodded, then turned her broad back and led the dogs away, chatting to them brightly.

Mike Edwards was under the cab of a new Ford tractor unit when Davis arrived at the transport yard, his Aberdeen training shoes identifying him as readily as a fingerprint. Hearing the rasp of the watchdog's chain across cement he crawled out into the thin sunlight, rubbed a black, greased hand over his forehead, then raised it in amicable greeting.

An ex-Paratrooper, tall, blond, still evidently in trim, Edwards had left the army to fight freelance for a while in Biafra and Nigeria with Colonel Ajoukie. So far as Davis knew, that had been the limit of his mercenary activities but it was nevertheless understood that he was always ready to consider potential contracts. Indeed, like many other one-time soldiers of fortune, Edwards had never settled to a routine of steady, regular employment, and had never moved outside the military environment. What he had done was join the growing band of independent owner-drivers prepared to transport heavy goods anywhere in the world, characteristically selecting the lucrative but treacherous run down to the Middle East.

Davis calculated that his practical knowledge of Arab States, together with his mechanical skills, might prove invaluable. Edwards possessed, moreover, a likeable and easy-going manner and a remarkably even temperament: qualities which could well be appreciated in the weeks ahead. Davis hoped, optimistically, that Edwards' presence would act as a kind of ballast for the rest of the team, knitting their disparate and volatile personalities together.

The two men walked slowly across the yard and entered the small, grey building, constructed out of breeze-blocks, which Edwards used as an office. It was empty except for a filing

47

cabinet, an old workbench, a telephone and a copy of 'May-fair'. There were two chairs. Davis thumbed through the magazine, rolled a cigarette and told Edwards there was the possibility of a job. Would he be interested?

Edwards smiled and looked out of the cracked window at the peaceful, sunlit yard. Beyond it he could see a corner of rural Surrey, the same uneven, autumnal patchwork of fields and fences he had been looking at for the past five weeks, bored to death.

"How much and how soon?"

Davis told him. Both of them knew he couldn't say more, for the moment.

Edwards paused, scratched his head, drummed his fingers on the top of the workbench. He smiled again.

"Fine. I'm in. Just give me a call."

"Better go home and pack," Davis said.

The two men shook hands solemnly.

An hour later, Davis put a call through to a number in Manchester. He was in luck. On the third ring the receiver was lifted and a familiar voice said,

"Hello. Johnson."

"Hi, Pat — it's Tom."

"Tom . . ."

"Look, Michael and I have a job going. Are you in?"

"When's the off?"

"Probably within the next twenty-four hours, certainly within the next forty-eight."

"Right," Johnson said flatly. "I'll catch the four-thirty from here. Be with you about nine, if that's okay?"

Davis grinned, invisibly.

"Yeah. Good boy, Pat."

He put the phone down. His first two choices! Perhaps the whole operation was going to be similarly blessed with luck. He had, after all, half expected Pat to be out of the country. The last rumour had placed him in Rhodesia, but he could in truth have been anywhere. He made a habit of disappearing, rather like a terrorist periodically going to ground, but apparently without as much cause, the cause being temperamental rather than political. Davis had taken a chance, phoning his mistress's home rather than his wife's (for he changed his mistress regularly too), but the gamble had paid off.

Pat was more than just a useful addition to the group. Also a product of the British Army (though a Commando rather than a Para) he was, in Davis's estimation, one of the best mercenaries in the business now that most of the old guard had retired. A few years older than the rest, his experience of warfare and ability to survive were almost legendary. He had fought with Ajoukie and Hoare and Callan. He had surfaced, at one time or another, in most of the wars, large and small, which had characterized an uncertain age. Violently anti-Communist (like so many freelance fighters) he had ritually engaged that enemy — through its satellites and acolytes — in shanty towns and cities and jungle clearings throughout the world. It was not a self-appointed mission but it was, at least to Davis, almost an obsession, a compunction which retirement could never resolve as it had for many of the others, his contemporaries in the perpetuity of war.

Johnson was a serious, sober, and dedicated professional, perfectly well acquainted with all the sophisticated (but sometimes rusticated) weaponry at the disposal of the modern mercenary. Personally rather reserved (so much so that he could, at times, appear shy and awkward), he was essentially a lone wolf with only the trappings of a precarious sociability. In another time, and on a different continent, Davis reflected, Johnson might well have been an outlaw, obeying the same private moral code and always contemptuous of normal social bonds and habits. In a way, of course, that was what he remained, an outlaw in uniform, a hired gun. The longevity of his career, in sharp contrast to the brevity of an outlaw's life, was therefore, perhaps, a tribute to a new sophistication, a sharper instinct, a greater deference to the iron laws of possibility — or, for that matter, merely a reminder of how far things had changed. After all, yesterday's outlaws were today's popular heroes, more sympathetically remembered than the

49

agents of law and order who hunted and removed them. But free-lance fighters now were simply dogs of war — or even, if it came to that, whores of war — unpopular, unrecognised individuals whose reputation would not even be redeemed by history. It might have been said of Johnson that he had been born on the wrong side of history; born at a moment when the outlaw was no more than a sentimental memory, and when conformity, rather than the impulse to take risks and step outside the conventions, was the social expectation.

Davis, however, had other expectations, and a professional admiration for the gaunt and reticent and rootless man, who would have fought at the Alamo with his fellow soldiers of fortune, had he been alive to take the chance. Davis could recall, in fact, only one flaw of any significance, and that was physical rather than psychological. Johnson limped slightly on his left foot, although the limp was barely detectable unless he was tired. Nevertheless the limp was a product of a genuine injury, a missing toe summarily removed by a shot-gun blast. Another English mercenary, a well-known figure, had himself executed the primitive punishment after discovering that Johnson had raped a young African girl. Several of the man's colleagues had at the time reacted to the incident with private revulsion, objecting to the display of cavalier morality, but curiously Johnson had both accepted the punishment and been changed by it. He no longer regarded casual sexual satisfaction as one of the spoils of war. He made no issue out of it but it clearly remained a stiff, unbroken principle, like a personal promise of which he carried, like a knotted handkerchief, the reminder. And Davis, though personally untouched by such a principle, nevertheless admired him for it, after a fashion.

But for the moment he dismissed it and, well-pleased, went upstairs to pack a few necessary changes of clothing into a light canvas bag. He came down when he heard the phone ringing. It was Christie, from Aldershot, who also sounded pleased with himself.

"I've signed Crofts and Duncan," he announced, as if,

Davis thought wryly, they were expensive football players and he a successful scout. Davis checked the names against the list in front of him.

"What about Wardell?" he cut in sharply.

"Disappeared. Christ knows where! Up North somewhere."

"Pity." Davis felt genuinely disappointed. "And Jordan?"

There was a long pause at the other end of the line, long enough for the question to be repeated.

"Jordan's dead," Christie said at last, in a voice devoid of emphasis.

"What? How?"

"I don't know." The response was almost sullen in its unwillingness. "A personal grudge, or something. He was found in his flat with his head caved in. Shagging someone's wife, I suppose."

"Or something!" Davis, unlike Christie, had known Jordan for ten years. Once, in an unfamiliar and burnt landscape, the Scotsman had extracted a bullet from his arm with an old penknife and, for anaesthetic, a bottle of whisky. Davis had never forgotten.

"Davis?"

"Yes."

"Are you telling me that Crofts and Duncan won't do? I thought we agreed."

Davis had never met either. He thought of Jordan as he checked their status, and ran a thin blue line across his name.

"They're SAS," he said. "Right?"

"Bloody right! Crofts was in Derry and on that train job in Holland. Duncan commanded an anti-terrorist squad and saw action in Borneo."

"They'll do, then." Davis felt sour. "It's up to you. But," he couldn't help adding, "do you know how they are . . . without the whole of the fucking British army behind them?"

Christie, tired from travelling and equally disappointed, exploded with anger.

"Davis, what the fuck has gone wrong with you?"

51

"Nothing's gone wrong with me. I got Edwards and Johnson, that's all."

"Well, fuck it, I'll get someone else, if you don't want SAS."

"No," Davis collected his thoughts. The inclusion of two SAS men wouldn't make any difference, even if he did believe that they weren't always the best-suited to mercenary work, but quarrelling with Christie might. "No, it's okay. It's fine. Are they coming back with you?"

"Yes." Christie's tone had also mollified. "We'll be there sometime tonight."

"Have you made contact with Hoffman?"

As he spoke, Davis heard the pips going and waited for Christie to insert another coin.

"No. I was wondering if you could call him with the names and find out about the tickets. You know how to do it?"

"Yes."

"Good. We'll drop the stuff off at Gatwick tomorrow morning anyway, as planned. See you later."

This time, Christie put the phone down first. Davis held the receiver in his hand for a moment, remembering certain things, especially his short, three-week long affair with Jordan's wife Nancy. Eventually, and probably after many similar episodes, she had left Jordan. He was a hard man but that night he had wept — sitting on Davis's sofa with his red, swollen eyes and his lost, desolate expression. Cast in the role of comforter, Davis had felt more like a dishonest friend, and yet he had also, curiously, found himself in sympathy with Jordan's enraged and caustic attack on women in general: their voraciousness, their selfishness and their vanity. Jordan's bitter, self-pitying words expressed a common sense, and the drunker Davis had become the stronger the conviction grew that Nancy Jordan, like some Medusa, had enticed then abused them both, as complacently as if she'd won them at a raffle.

Were Jordan's crimes any more, or less, forgivable? Had he been slaughtered by some jealous husband — or was it a contract? Mercenaries are never short of enemies, even in their own camp, even among their closest acquaintances. Wars leave many scores to settle and many wounds unhealed. Davis himself had not been untouched by the incestuous habit of revenge and retribution: had been telephoned, late one night, and promised the shallowest of graves for an old mistake. He had ignored the warning. He could not afford the luxury of constant vigilance — and the threat had melted away. Had it been the same for Jordan? Or had his sudden, violent death been domestic and ordinary?

Davis put the receiver down on its crook, lit a cigarette, and went upstairs to finish packing.

Two hours later Tippett arrived, parking the Scimitar behind Davis's rather more battered Jaguar, its boot full of equipment. The shopping spree had been a success. Tippett had acquired four radio sets — not inexpensive Japanese models, but the type of set frequently used by the American police which could receive and transmit over a five-mile radius and whose performance, crucially, was unaffected by the steel reinforcing used in the construction of multi-storey and accommodation blocks. He also showed Davis a set of four spare crystals, mauve-coloured instead of the grey ones already installed in the radios, in case, he pointed out, they found any need to change the receiving and transmitting frequency once they were in the bank, thus preserving the privacy of their conversations. Davis was agreeably surprised by Tippett's foresight, but said nothing, moving on to the seven sets of webbing harness, each complete with water bottles and combat medical kits. Opening each in turn he checked through the contents: a packet of five syringes each prefilled with anti-biotics, two dressings, various bottles of pills (anti-malaria, dysentery, water-purifiers) and an ampoule of morphine. He held one of the morphine capsules between two fingers and looked up, quizzically.

"Courtesy of the British army," Tippett said, with a wink.

Perhaps more unexpected, however, were the two American-made bullet-proof vests. Extremely light in weight (at about seven pounds) the vests could stop almost any round

53

from a traditional service weapon, including the very heavy Magnum and 7-62 NATO rounds.

Charitably, Tippett handed one across. Davis refused it.

"A friendly supplier in the States already sent me one," he explained. "They have a magazine over there offering everything from bazookas to army surplus jets."

"Free enterprise," Tippett said drily. "Can we get a B52?"

Davis ignored the comment.

"Give the jacket to Christie," he said. "He ought to wear one all the fucking time, even in the bath." Davis thought sharply of Jordan.

Tippett tidied away the equipment.

"You don't like him?" he said, phrasing it as a question.

Davis shook his head. "That's right. I don't."

"You don't have to. Like him, I mean."

"No, but I may have to trust him, and I'm not sure that I trust him any more than Hoffman."

Tippett sighed heavily, as if at the repetition of an over-familiar song.

"It doesn't matter a fuck if you trust Hoffman or not," he said bluntly. "He knows what he's talking about, and he's paying us money. It's just a contract."

Davis stood up.

"Hoffman's a liar, you know that. The bank knows nothing about this whole operation, otherwise we'd have keys to that vault and not a lecture from a nervous little man Hoffman somehow produces out of his pocket. Whatever is in those boxes, he wants for himself. The rest is shit."

"Okay . . ." Tippett opened out his palms in a gesture of agreement. "So what? That just makes him a mercenary too, doesn't it? Like you and me. Like a lot of people, trying to get what they want. I agree that the rest is shit."

Davis smiled, partially acknowledging the obvious.

"I just don't want to die for that bastard," he finished, the smile broadening to a generous grin.

"Have you talked to him today?" Tippett wondered. "That bastard."

"An hour ago."

"And?"

"And," Davis said, "it's on. The freight plane leaves for Cyprus at six-thirty tomorrow morning. We've got to get you and all this stuff to Gatwick by six."

Tippett, a notoriously late sleeper, pulled a long face.

"What about picking up the tickets?"

"You'll have to do that as well," replied Davis, not bothering to disguise a satisfied smile. "Hoffman has got everything ready." He extracted a piece of paper from his pocket, handing it over. "These are the numbers Hoffman wanted. Add yours."

"What about you?"

"The flights are booked for the day after, morning and afternoon."

"Seems stupid not to all go on that plane tomorrow," Tippett said.

"Does it? I imagine we'd find it hard to convince the authorities we were all going on holiday on a freight plane! Or would you like to be on television again?"

For a moment they both remembered, vividly and with discomfort, the exodus to Angola in the glare of television lights, the accusing cameras and questions and jibes. It had even prompted a book called *The Whores of War* which Davis kept in his lavatory.

Tippett said nothing.

"Christie and the two SAS blokes will catch the first flight. I'll be on the second with Edwards and Johnson," Davis explained.

"Two SAS?" Tippett was momentarily puzzled. "What about Mac?"

Davis visibly hesitated.

"Jordan's away somewhere. Christie couldn't find him."

"Shit!"

"Yes."

Davis heard a heavy lorry rumbling past the front of the house. Its headlights briefly, brightly illuminated the uncurtained window before it accelerated away roughly, probably carrying a group of regular soldiers home from their exercises.

"And Hoffman's got all my stuff already?" Tippett said, a trace of disbelief in his voice. The fact that he was leaving the next day had evidently made him realise, as if for the first time, the precipitous momentum of the whole operation, even compared with the scramble to Angola.

Davis was reassuring. Hoffman had apparently organised everything, including the ice machine. He'd arranged it all. They were really rather small, insignificant cogs in an elaborate machine that had already been started, that had already been running before Hoffman had even approached them. And, like pieces of machinery, they would simply be transported and placed wherever they were required.

"I told Hoffman you'd be there at seven," he told Tippett. "You'd better get off."

"Thanks," Tippett said, "I was just going."

"See you back here in about two hours."

Tippett put his coat back on, stuffing his hands into the pockets. He looked down at Davis.

"It's going to be fucking great," he said. "Fucking magnificent."

"If you say so . . ."

Tippett let himself out into the cold, bitter air.

Davis went over to the window. There was a full moon, slightly pink in colour, set in a deep blue and darkening sky. In two days time he would be surveying it from a different angle, from another country. It was a satisfying feeling, expansive and gratifying. He tried to think of the money, the reasons behind it all, of being rich, extravagantly, strangely rich. The idea should have meant something to him, but it seemed unreal, unlikely, curiously absurd. He knew he would have gone anyway, for a smaller promise, a lower purse, would have gone to fight, to risk himself, because the instinct was as compulsive as sex and sometimes even more so.

His reservations, his doubts, seemed to wither away comprehensively as he stood there, at the point of departure, knowing (as he had known all the time in Angola) that he would survive. He was bound to survive. In war it was always possible to survive, no matter what. And, on the whole, it was a good team, not the haphazard collection of Americans and Portuguese and Angolans that Callan had directed, that often composed, in fact, a mercenary army. There would only be seven of them (against how many, he thought, both Christian and Moslem?) but it was always surprising how effective a few professional and particularly motivated soldiers could be. War was inevitably a psychological just as much as a military exercise, and if a soldier of fortune had one advantage it was precisely his instinctive habit of firing first, as a reflex, without waiting to be sure, or for orders, or for justification. Of course in Africa it had been different and easier: the myth of the white soldier had still, curiously, protected them, allowed them an importance out of all proportion to their numbers and the ineptitude of their leaders. In Beirut, he supposed, there would be no such allowance, and no useful myth. Nevertheless there would be no ineptitude, no contradictory orders (one of Callan's specialities), no confusions, and perhaps, after all, a necessary myth — that of survival, in spite of everything.

Davis smiled at the full moon. It seemed to him, at that moment, somehow so full of promise.

That same evening Hoffman had just finished showering when the telephone rang. He answered it in the bedroom, lying across the blue bedclothes, without bothering to take a towel. He pushed his wet hair back, out of his eyes.

It was a transatlantic call, but the operator at the other end of the line asked him to wait. He waited impatiently for well over a minute. Then an unfamiliar male voice said,

"Hi, Martin! How's it going?"

"I'm fine," Hoffman replied. "Everything's fine."

"That's great. We're glad to hear it. Bobby's been asking after you."

"It's nice of him to worry." Hoffman began to rub an edge of the rough bedspread over his wet skin.

"What's that, Martin?"

"I said he shouldn't worry. I picked up all the articles he wanted at Christies. Reserve price."

"He'll be pleased, Martin. Really. You know how the dollar is. I'll tell him."

The ingratiating voice paused, probably to allow the man a moment to consult his notes. In the privacy of his English bedroom, Martin Hoffman gestured angrily, almost petulantly. He didn't like the familiar tone. It was unnecessary and provocative. He wondered what the man looked like. Fresh-faced, light-skinned, alertly stupid with small, water-blue eyes and a thin, arrogant, pretty mouth. Ex-Harvard, something like that, with a carefully crumpled suit that looked more lived-in than it was. Why in God's name, Hoffman thought, do they still put people like this on the phone to me? He would have liked to tell him that, but he couldn't: the conversations were always taped.

"Oh," the voice began again, brightly, "and how's Davy's arm? We wanted him to see someone about it, fix it up. Bobby wanted him to see a specialist, but you know what he's like? He can be stubborn."

"Yes. I told him. But doctors are expensive and so is insurance. Anyway, he finally found someone, a good Jewish doctor, who fixed him up okay."

"That's good. So, everything's fine with you?"

"Sure. I'm surprised that Bobby should be concerned."

The voice ignored the implication.

"He's only worried for your sake, Martin. Really. You're on a very tight schedule, we appreciate that, and I guess Bobby is concerned in case he's expecting too much. How you're finances, by the way?"

Hoffman grimaced. The man was clumsy as well as patronizing.

58

"I'll get to the bank next week," he said stiffly. "I can live on traveller's cheques." Despite everything, he was rather pleased with that. "Well, give my regards to Bobby — and your mother, now. Bye, bye."

After a moment of silence, the phone went dead. Hoffman turned over and lay with his wet hair on the pillow, his eyes closed, the momentary satisfaction of the small joke more than offset by the irritation he felt, had always felt, at being powerless, at someone else's beck and call.

Hoffman was not the man he appeared, had not risen by his own skills or by good fortune or by virtue of a system which promoted and encouraged the sons of the poor, the dispossesed, to aim for the highest offices. He had simply been used, embraced and shaped by the system itself, been virtually fed and clothed by it so that, as recompense, it required both his submission and his service. Certainly he was clever — clever enough, in fact, to have won two scholarships, a University place, then another at business school — had clawed his way from an unpromising beginning into a banking career, but even then he was neither independent nor satisfied. He wanted to cut a figure in the world. He had worked hard for more years than he had anticipated, and still he was years away from Wall Street, from privilege and power, from a state of luxury.

So it had happened that, by recommendation and chance encounter, he had become involved with a small and newly-established government department which monitored and investigated the financial status and accountability of any company brought to its attention. Hoffman had not been a reluctant recruit — it seemed, if anything, a worthwhile and lucrative investment of his time — and since he was soon being placed on the board of directors of some influential concerns he could also feel, with satisfaction, that his career had suddenly blossomed. He was a good investigator. He had a flair for uncovering the best-hidden secrets, for compromising those whose personal ambitions corroded and corrupted their companies' policies. He liked to turn over the loose stones and

59

see the vermin and the lice crawling out into the sunlight.

He was well-paid, and soon he was operating overseas, moving from country to country, company to company, enjoying the illusion of his independence, his image as a man of the world. Then, with remarkable abruptness, the illusion had been shattered. His paymasters had co-opted him on to the Board of a company called Rawlinson Electronics, a Chicago-based firm with subsidiaries all over the world. Hoffman visited them all, had done his job with characteristic thoroughness, interviewed personally all the directors (they included a number of prominent politicians), many of its customers and scrutinized the accounts. The company was booming, and more than that it was healthy, profitable, expansionist, and sound. Hoffman could discover virtually nothing to discredit its operation or compromise its reputation. His report, unusually, was almost glowing, though he was careful to hedge it about with considerations. Nevertheless it was rejected. He was told he was being naive, simple-minded and unprofessional. His brief was not to exonerate, to excuse, to justify, but to incriminate; Rawlinson Electronics had to be driven out of business within the year.

Hoffman's reaction to this information was, at first, one of resentment and refusal. He was being compromised, lied to and forced to recognise the cheap worthlessness of his own position. Of course, if there was some good reason for the company and its policies to be brought under wider public scrutiny, that was another matter, but one on which he should have been consulted. An intemperate phone call to Washington, however, had produced no such explanation or apology. He was merely informed, bluntly, that the agency for which he worked was not accountable to its investigators, nor itself open to investigation or query. Hoffman was being paid to do a job, not to question its efficacy or purpose. If he felt, as a result, that he was being unfairly and morally compromised, he had only to say so and his contract would be terminated at once.

That evening, Hoffman had carefully drafted his letter of

resignation. It seemed to him remarkable that they should continue to expect him to work for an agency whose aims and intentions remained obscure and private, and possibly political. No doubt there were reasons behind their reticence and secrecy (features of many American governmental operations), but both his arrogance and vanity were injured by their failure to conceive of allowing him some access to their inner cabinets.

The letter took two hours to write but only a few seconds to destroy. After all, there were things, privileges and opportunities, Hoffman prized more highly than his personal integrity. He could not easily think of throwing everything over for the sake of a principle, and in any case he had little choice. There was nothing to go back to.

In the morning he took a flight back to Hong Kong, his conscience pacified, his vanity restored. In another month he had prepared a second report, less substantive, more conjectural, which was accepted, despite its insufficiencies. And after that Hoffman made few mistakes, so few that his brief was extended to cover a miscellaneous range of activities, from arranging currency deals to occasional meetings with the representatives of foreign governments (some of them in exile) who required practical, financial aid. Some of these dealings appeared to Hoffman to be proper and reasonable; others he supposed or recognised to be problematic. Either way, he was not concerned, although he continued to feel frustrated that his power was implied rather than real: simply a gift from his employers, a fiction they had created on his behalf.

The Beirut operation was different only because Hoffman had never before had to deal directly and personally with mercenary labour. The fact that he was trusted to do so (since the agency had already indicated the importance of the assignment) should perhaps have been flattering, but in many ways their introduction merely complicated his arrangements and increased his personal liabilities. Should something go wrong — and he was enough of a realist to accept the probability — then his portion of guilt would be self-evident. They were allowing him no measure of self-protection, yet at the same time they were employing their habitual device of keeping him, if not in the dark then in the twilight zone of limited apprehension, particular objectives.

Moreover, he did not especially enjoy having to deal with the sort of men whom he had summoned, as it were, from the underworld of social life. Of course he recognised their value, and the purpose of selecting an English team (though Sneiger had suggested it), yet he felt compromised at having to deal with them directly and personally, as if it tainted him. These seedy and secret meetings contradicted his cultivated image, just as they threatened his security. He disliked even more, though again he had been made aware of its desirability, having to fashion that special and particular arrangement with Christie. Sneiger had been responsible for the idea, and as usual with good reason: he had found something out. Christie, it seemed, had made a few unusual bargains in the course of an admittedly chequered career. Like Hoffman himself (like God knows how many others, Hoffman had glibly reflected) he was not altogether what he seemed. The recruiter of men and arms for one side had, from time to time, been a consultant, a watch-dog, for the other, aborting some of the very coups he'd helped to arrange. Ironically enough, it was British Intelligence, now often but mistakenly under-rated, which had discovered the unseemly fact, but it was the invaluable Sneiger who had finally managed to put it to good use. Christie had therefore been bluntly informed that his presence on the team was a requirement of his participation. It was, effectively, as simple as that, but it constituted at the very least a measure of insurance. Hoffman had not been prepared to trust the others for a moment, nor was Sneiger's presence alone a guarantee of their behaviour. Blackmailing Christie, tying his star to that of Hoffman's rather than Davis's, made a promise of co-operation, just as it ensured that Hoffman's head would not be the only one to roll if things went wrong.

More even than that, however, was Hoffman's acid satisfaction at having sent another backroom boy to the front. In some respects, as he could see well enough, he and Christie were of a kind: organisers, manipulators, politicians. And if he had been forced to descend into the arena where reputations were muddied and fouled, he didn't see why the same shouldn't be true for Christie, the little man with such big ambitions. Christie was out of his depth, but didn't know it yet. He was like a small-time gangster in a bad movie: full of talk and swagger and bravado. Hoffman doubted whether he could keep it up. He was being sent into hell, where bluster counted for nothing. No doubt it was malicious to relish his potential discomfort, but then discomfort, perhaps of a temporary kind, was the least of Christie's worries. Hoffman had not the slightest conscience, in any case, about what happened to the Englishman.

5

When the freight plane carrying Michael Tippett and the consignment of chemicals and plant touched down at Limasol airport, Cyprus, Makmoud was already there to meet it. His truck was unobtrusively parked at one end of the apron, just inside the perimeter fence, and as the small plane taxied towards it he climbed out of the cab and began to unroll the heavy sheet of tarpaulin that covered the wooden floor-boards.

Makmoud, equipped with order papers supplied by Chamoun, had arrived much too early, in case the airport officials decided to question them. His apprehensions, however, were unfounded: he had been waved through onto the strip of tarmac after only the most cursory of examinations, and although the truck had been accompanied by two officers wearing side arms, they seemed more pre-occupied with keeping the area clear of normal airport traffic. Their behaviour, together with official acquiescence over custom formalities, rather increased his sense of self-importance, once his nervousness had abated, and Makmoud was left to speculate on his major contribution to the great adventure ahead.

He was also interested to see this foreign mercenary and was pleased, upon introduction, to discover a man who seemed tall and strong, confident without being too arrogant; a man who lacked the supercilious qualities of the British soldiers he had met in the past. Makmoud had never truly lost his contempt for the British army, but this was different. He knew that this man belonged to no army or occupying force, and was not to

64

blame for the past. In some ways, indeed, he was here to redeem it.

Together they unloaded the materials from the plane, indifferently observed by the uniformed men, and then Makmoud rolled the tarpaulin back into place. The men at the gates waved them through, and soon he was driving cautiously through the bustling town, these days full of rich Lebanese refugees escaping from the fighting over the water. Once outside he turned the truck towards Pathos, before turning again some miles later towards the interior and the mountains. Now the roads were not at all good. They were rough, uncemented and full of cracks and holes, but at least they were virtually empty of traffic. And the suspension on the truck was good. Makmoud started to drive faster, skidding round the larger holes in the uneven surface. He didn't want to waste time.

He talked, as he drove, about Cyprus, pointing out villages to his quiet passenger, small and poor though they were. After the rains the landscape was green and fertile, just as he had heard an English spring might be. There were wild flowers in the tall grass and everything looked renewed and freshly painted, except the houses. Even the bare white hills and the carob trees, bleached by the evening sun, seemed less severe, greener, more pleasant.

Makmoud was delighted that, in describing all this, his English did not let him down. Not often did he have to search his brain for the right word. So, in truth, he was surprised that the handsome mercenary rarely answered him, turned his head, or asked him questions. He would have liked a real conversation. And then, at last, when the man did speak it was only to say, in a cold, clear voice:

"How much further?"

Makmoud pretended not to be offended. He smiled back.

"A few miles only. Not now. Soon. Over there!"

He pointed through the windscreen, out at the remote blue distance. The truck hit another hole, jolted, and swung to the right before the Lebanese brought it sharply back onto the road, frowning.

"Slow down!" the mercenary said.

Makmoud just avoided another and larger pothole. He shook his head.

"No good," he said, easing his foot off the accelerator. "Bad roads. Always."

"Then go more slowly."

He resented the Englishman's officious tone, with its hint of patronage, as though he were stupid. He put his foot down again and the truck bounced across a series of sharp corrugations.

"Stop!"

"What?" Makmoud, surprised, looked across quickly. "Pardon?"

"Stop the fuckin' truck!" The mercenary was shouting at him too loudly. He stopped the truck slowly and looked around for the trouble. The road was empty. There were no cars, or people, or houses, just trees, flowers, and the red sun sinking behind the hills.

The mercenary, however, was already pulling back the edges of the tarpaulin at the back of the truck. Makmoud went to join him, examining the large, dark green carbuoys of acid questioningly, wondering if they could furnish an explanation. He looked up. He could see that Tippett was really angry for there was accusation and anger in his eyes. Then the man started to curse and swear and shout at him again.

"You stupid bastard! You blind cunt! Don't you understand anything? Don't you know what this stuff is?"

Makmoud was polite. He said, yes, he did, he had seen it before.

"You could have killed us both, idiot!"

Makmoud shrugged his shoulders carefully. He was not a stupid man and it was an insult to be shouted at in this way. He went back and sat in the cab.

As they drove away he was conscious of the man glaring at him fiercely, watching him. It made him uncomfortable and he drove badly. The truck's right wheel caught the edge of a steep rut; it went up, then jolted down. Before he had time to

66

say anything Tippett, leaning over, pulled out the stop button with his left hand, grabbed the steering wheel with his right, and butted his head hard into Makmoud's face: the Lebanese could feel warm, thick blood running from his nostrils, bubbling over his chin.

Then, just as abruptly, the attack finished and the mercenary, his foot on the brake, brought the truck to a gentle stop. Makmoud, blinded by pain, shook his head slowly. He could hardly see. His face hurt badly, and when he held it back the blood went into his throat. After a while he opened the door of the truck, leaned out and vomited bile and blood over the backed road. But then the Englishman pulled him back inside and, without a word, helped to clean his face. Makmoud touched his nose to see if it was broken, for he had heard something crack loudly, as if the bone had splintered, and if the heavy bleeding had finally stopped. He felt confused and angry, and would certainly have killed the man had Chamoun not warned him to be careful. He swallowed another mouthful of clotted blood that tasted like his own pride and gazed harshly at Tippett, seeing at once how the man's mood had changed, that he was curiously calm, even looking slightly embarrassed. He offered Makmoud a cigarette, lighting it first, and the Lebanese tried to bury his resentment in the silence between them. He drove on slowly.

In half an hour they reached the house, a large, whitewashed villa set on a steep hillside, sheltered by carob and olive trees. The house was several miles from the nearest village and although still impressive, with its wide courtyard and palm trees and rows of shuttered windows, it was also showing the signs of neglect, the faded paintwork, the weeds forcing their way between the flagstones, the cracking plaster. But inside it was cool, dark and dry, and the faded elegance of the low-ceilinged, well-furnished rooms created a still sense of privilege and culture and repose.

Makmoud had only been to the house once before, and then many years previously, yet it had not changed, merely decayed a little for the absence of a human touch. He walked quickly through the marbled-floored, frescoed entrance hall, and entered a smaller room to the left. It was as he remembered it. There were great paintings in wide wooden frames, portraits and landscapes, chairs with elaborately carved backs and a polished mahogany table. Standing in the doorway he recalled his last and only visit, how the doors had been pushed open for him, and how, at once, he had seen General Grivas sitting at the head of that very table, with his boots resting upon its surface. Grivas, with his thick black moustache and glittering eyes had made him welcome, had even come forward, ceremoniously, to present the medal and commend him with such fine phrases that Makmoud had shivered with pleasure and fear, and afterwards wept. How he remembered it all, the phrases troubling the undisturbed silence of the elegant little room.

They died away and Makmoud went back outside to help the English mercenary unload his packages and carbuoys, carrying them behind the house to a concrete bunker hidden among the trees and now almost overgrown. As they worked, the silence was only broken by the sounds of the cicadas and the other man's cursory commands. Makmoud tried to be patient and careful for, like the mercenary's, his own temper was quick and violent. And what would Chamoun say if he disobeyed orders and killed him now, too early? It was simple. Chamoun would have him shot without compunction like a dog in the streets.

Two hours after his delayed arrival in Cyprus with Edwards and Johnson, Davis, nicely settled into his small but comfortable hotel bedroom and having established the whereabouts of the other group, was contacted by Hoffman's associate Robert Sneiger. Davis invited him to meet them as soon as possible at the hotel, then phoned Christie again and told him the arrangement. Christie promised to have everyone at the hotel by six o'clock.

Sneiger arrived ten minutes later. He was sweating profusely and holding a large, lilac handkerchief which he employed constantly to mop his brow. He also carried a battered attaché case from which, in the privacy of Davis's now crowded room, he produced plans and photographs of the bank and the surrounding buildings, and a number of maps of the area. He appeared to be confident and well-informed and answered each question with precise and thoughtful gravity, pointing out that the photographs, unlike the ones they had seen of the vault door, were several weeks old: they showed the bank at the time of its occupation by the Christian forces. Some of the surrounding buildings had been damaged by mortar fire and there was a certain quantity of rubble on the streets. Nevertheless the photographs showed groups of civilians standing in the doorways or walking along the pavements, threading their way through the maze of small, busy thoroughfares that seemed to lead the eye towards the large, imposing building which housed the bank.

"The streets are very narrow," Christie said, as the pictures were handed round. "There isn't another way in, is there?"

Sneiger shook his head.

"You don't have a choice," he said. "All the streets are very narrow, some of them may be blockaded, but you have to approach the bank from the front, along here," he indicated the street. "In any case, as you know, you will have an escort. Their job will be to guide you and clean up any pockets of resistance. Your concern is the bank itself."

Davis had been looking at another shot. He drew Sneiger's attention to the design of the building itself. It wouldn't, he considered, take many men to defend it successfully. He indicated the wide, Roman-style arch at the front of the bank.

"There's a courtyard through there?"

"Yes. A small, inner courtyard built around a fountain. The house once belonged to a rich Arab merchant and the bank retained many of the old features."

"How many men do they have?"

"In the vicinity? Perhaps a hundred. Of course it's hard to

69

be exact. We're hoping our shelling will draw many of them away."

"And in the bank?" Davis persisted.

"Who knows? Ten. Maybe thirty. We doubt that it's particularly heavily guarded. They control the whole area after all."

"The truth is, you're merely speculating," Edwards interrupted. "Isn't that right?"

The comment drew a thin, bleak smile from the American.

"Up to a point, of course. There are some things we don't know, but then we think we're covered for most eventualities. As I'm sure you appreciate, no operation of this kind is without its risks. We're naturally gambling on taking them by surprise, going in and out very fast and very efficiently. You have support. I don't think we can reasonably do more."

Davis grunted noncommittally and turned to the hand-drawn pictures of the bank's interior, showing the three open-plan floors together with the two identical, wide stone stair-cases, one at either end of the building. The floors were otherwise separated by rows of thick stone columns, preserved by the builders in their efforts to blend the old with the new. There was also a smaller and spiral staircase, situated on the third floor, which led up to the roof, and yet another on the ground floor.

"The vault is here," Sneiger pointed over his shoulder, "down these steps." He traced the route from the entrance hall to the vault with his finger. "There's bound to be a lot of debris around here. They must have tried several times to blast that door."

The other mercenaries filed past the table slowly and largely in silence, until Davis was certain that each of them had a good idea of the bank's layout.

He asked the American: "So, when do we go?"

"Tomorrow evening. A fishing boat from the harbour will take us across. Collect at nine o'clock on the old quay — you can't fail to find it, but I suggest you walk that way tonight — to the north of the city. I'll be there to meet you."

"Fine."

70

"Oh," Sneiger paused before opening the door, "we've found a truck for you. You'll have a day to work on it. I hope that's sufficient."

He closed the door quietly.

Tippett, standing in the bright, sterile bunker in the green shade, admired his handiwork and wiped the sweat running down his face. It was dawn — a fact he noticed for the first time — and pale sunshine had begun to filter through the two tiny windows, spiking the wooden bench and the wall behind it. Olive leaves rustled against the glass, the thick stems knotted rather than simply laced together, and a vaguely fresher air somehow found its way into the putrid-smelling cell.

He had worked all night, allowing Makmoud, who at first, in a characteristically incautious way, had been some help, to disappear to his bedroom in the early hours, but going on himself, carefully but mechanically, until, for a certain period, there was nothing more for him to do.

During the whole endless night he had only occasionally been conscious of the strain under which he was forced to work. Now, with the daylight, it seemed to affect his body like an arthritic attack, almost doubling him up with agony so that he had to lean heavily against the workbench, bleary-eyed and stiff and slightly chilled, as if the tension had kept him coldly rigid and calm throughout the night. He even felt older, as though the worst minutes, which had seemed to last, each one of them, for hours on end, had actually done so.

He could have done with a radio, but then it would have distracted his attention, relaxed his concentration. He had sometimes been aware of animal or bird noises outside the bunker, rustlings and strange, prolonged cries, but after a while he had forgotten to listen, gone back to his mixing, hearing nothing except the dull metallic rattle of the extractor unit. As he feared, it had not been sufficient to save his impaired lungs from the affects of the poisonous fumes. He had felt the familiar tightening across his chest and now he found himself wheezing like an asthmatic and coughing: a painful, hacking cough that brought up great gobs of discoloured phlegm.

Nevertheless, and despite the discomfort, he had sufficient reason to be pleased with the night's work. It had started when he poured the thick, treacle-like fuming nitric acid into a large glass mixing bowl, then stirred the malevolent liquid carefully with a long glass rod, before adding a small quantity of sulphuric acid. The glass thermometer, with a piece of red tape wound around its upper graduations, had told him when the mixture was becoming too volatile; once the mercury touched the tape, the mixture would explode. To cool it, he packed ice around the outside of the bowl, constantly replenishing the supply from the machine beside him.

Throughout the night the mercury had slipped up and down the scale like a car on a Coney Island switchback ride, just occasionally threatening the thin band of red before dropping down again to safety. Finally, an hour ago, Tippett had been able to pour the viscous, grey and still only half-prepared mixture into a number of large storage jars, set at the back of the long bench. He looked at them now with all the curiosity of detachment. In a few hours he would have to return, transferring the grease to smaller tablet jars, each topped with a cap of water, an effective shock absorber. Then, after a while, the liquid would slowly change colour, indicating the culmination of the process. At that point, it would be nearly ready for use, with only the glycerine to add, though that process remained the most volatile of all.

For the moment, however, the mercenary could sleep, tranquilized by exhaustion. He returned to the house, just as the sun's warmth began to permeate the still air. He did not trouble about over-sleeping (Makmoud had orders to wake him), nor did he anticipate anything but a deep, untroubled and much-needed rest. Yet, as he slept, in a warm, whitewashed bedroom, Tippett's waking dreams left him soaked with the cold sweat of an oppressive, incalculable fear.

As arranged the other six mercenaries gathered on the quiet

quayside at nine o'clock, casually dressed, but feeling nevertheless conspicuous as they looked back at the clustering,
domestic lights of Larnaka or gazed out at the gentle swell of
the sea, hearing it lap against the old wooden posts of the jetty.
It was a mild, fragrant evening, cooled by a breeze that fanned
in from the sea and punctuated by the spirited shouts of young
boys playing along the high harbour walls.

Sneiger arrived ten minutes later, breathlessly apologizing.
He was not alone. With him were two Lebanese, similar
enough in looks and build to have been twins, who were introduced as the group's guides and interpreters. The mercenaries
were more interested to notice that both were armed with AK
47s, the Russian assault rifles, carrying them openly and, in a
manner they were soon to be familiar with, rather jauntily, like
umbrellas. Davis found their presence disconcerting rather
than reassuring. Clearly disinclined to talk, except to one
another, they appeared less like interpreters than watch dogs,
carefully shepherding their charges over the vulnerable
waters. They stood slightly apart from the mercenaries,
despite Sneiger's inept promptings. Eventually he too fell
silent, standing awkwardly between the two parties, reflex-
ively mopping his brow with the lilac handkerchief.

Very soon they saw the dark shadow of the fishing boat cutting the calm waters just beyond the lip of the land. It
approached slowly, showing no lights, eventually settling
alongside, its sides chafing against the cement wall. Less than
five minutes later it had slipped its moorings and was heading
back out to sea, its ancient engine complaining under the ruck
of the deeper waters.

The mercenaries had arranged themselves at the stern. They
sat on crates and dry coils of rope in the confined space, their
harnesses stacked between them, while the two Lebanese,
silent, unobtrusive but vigilant, squatted on their haunches,
their backs to the cabin. Darkness folded them in, as if it kept
their secret, ferrying them to the other side. Clouds obscured a
distant and reddish moon, parting occasionally, like the boat's
wake, to allow cold shafts of light through. Sometimes they

caught and illuminated the boat, like the inquisitive, harsh, probing beam of a distant search-light.

Christie, since arriving in Cyprus, had said little, except to introduce the two aloof but polite SAS men. Now, pressed in between Edwards and Davis, he began to talk, as though easing some inner tension. He told them that his wife had recently given birth to a baby girl, his second child, and that he was having a new house built, on the banks of a river, in a secluded village in Sussex.

"It's really for the wife and kids," he explained. "Just in case, you know . . . I wanted to leave them something. They can always sell the house. It'll be worth a bit." His voice trailed off uncomfortably. "What do you make of those guys?" with his eyes he indicated the two statue-like Lebanese. Davis shrugged.

"What about them?"

Christie turned away, as if to examine the churning, glittering water of the boat's wake. Watching the movement, Davis had the sensation of watching an old suspicion take shape as a certainty. The pantomime of unease suggested, just as in a hundred grainy films, a young soldier about to enter the theatre of war for the first time. Of course, Christie was no longer a young man (he must have been in his late thirties), but the raw ends of his nerves were showing. His expression was tense, as though he was being careful to keep the muscles under control, and if there were as yet no flickerings of fear in his eyes, there was, behind their glaze, a remoteness which implied a desire to look on more familiar things than the drab little boat and the colourless sea.

Davis had to repress an inclination to put Christie to the test: to challenge his experience, his reasons for joining them. He would either have made the man look foolish in front of the others, or been made to look foolish himself. Christie might well be a stranger to these kinds of conditions but he was clearly no stranger to an argument. What was more, Christie, though somehow closer to Hoffman, had never asserted any of the privileges of that intimacy. He had easily given over the leadership to Davis, submerging himself within the collective identity of the group. However much he had done so as a means of protecting himself, it was still in Davis's interests to maintain the cohesive spirit behind the enterprise. To pick a quarrel at this time would be compromising, and might cast a shadow over his own judgment which would be difficult to dispel.

He lit a cigarette and stretched out his legs. The smell of the tobacco failed to disguise the strong smell of fish, for that scent appeared to have seeped into the very fabric of the creaking vessel. Somehow it was not unpleasant. There was something even vaguely, absurdly romantic about the situation, again with that quality of an old black and white film, a quality of unreality, as if an unseen director might at any moment make an appearance and bring the scene to a sudden close. But just as there was no God to observe them, so there was no director in the wings. The sense of unreality — heightened, curiously, by the men with guns who watched over them — would disappear imperceptibly, perhaps, once this crossing was over.

Davis looked across at Johnson. He wondered if, after so many wars, each man became, to a degree, less real, fading into each other like the absurd sequences of a dream. Johnson had a purpose, after all, only in the sense that those Japanese soldiers, left behind in the jungles long after another war had finished, had a purpose. They, like him, continued to arm themselves against an idea, but one that had abandoned its military dressing, as if by agreement. Johnson, of course, thought that he still had an enemy and that the enemy was always and everywhere at war, whether in Cambodia, or South Africa, or on the streets of Paris. But perhaps he was wrong. The enemy, if it was Marxism, existed as a state of mind, or lay buried in Highgate cemetery, out of reach of a stray bullet. Like those Japanese soldiers, Johnson was stranded on the wrong side of history, left behind in the jungles of an abandoned war.

Edwards nudged his shoulder, bringing him back to notice that the sky was lighter, clearer, and the sea an even lighter and different blue. The noise of the boat's engine sounded ferocious; it sputtered sickly against the heaving swell.

"Look," Edwards directed. Ahead he could see a long black risen mass of land. "Do you think this fucking boat will make it?"

"How do you feel?" Davis said.

"Cold. I hate water. Do you realise this trip has taken the whole fucking night?"

"Are the others sleeping?"

"They're frozen to fucking death." Edwards rubbed his hands together brusquely. "Is that the Lebanon?"

"How do I know? Perhaps it's Saudi Arabia, or Cornwall. Those bastards haven't slept." The interpreters gazed at them sightlessly, gently, carressingly rubbing the barrels of their guns.

Edwards grunted miserably. After a while he said:

"And there's just seven of us!"

Davis, without replying, attempted to interpret the tone.

"The fucking magnificent seven," Edwards said. "God Almighty!"

The land mass continued to rise stubbornly out of the water, creating a nearer, thicker horizon. And then the tip of the mildly glowing, pale sun appeared beyond it, a crescent of orange emerging warmly from the bleak, hard landscape. They watched it, some of them roused from impatient slumbers, until the boat, after skirting an inhospitable beach, brought them finally ashore.

They found two battered VW minibuses, their engines idling, waiting at the top of a gently sloping field. Sneiger, once more concerned to establish a measure of authority, ushered them fussily aboard, his eyes heavy with sleep. Sneiger's peremptory commands, so different from his earlier and nervous civilities, grated badly on the mercenaries' nerves. More than they, he seemed an unlikely and unsuitable figure to have been washed ashore here, in this armed and violent land, and his loud gestures did nothing to create sympathy. Davis, at least, was privately satisfied that his efforts to ingratiate himself with their 'interpreters' and then with the two sullen-looking bus drivers appeared equally fruitless and embarrassing. But Sneiger seemed oblivious to the slights. His neat, safari-like suit, evidently new, preposterously inappropriate, made him seem, in some ways, like a minor civil servant trying to cope with an illegal landing of unwelcome immigrants. The sense of unreality came flooding back upon Davis, amusing him as it simultaneously angered him, as the old buses bounced and rattled across the deep ruts of the green and peaceful field. This was not Sneiger's place any more than it was Hoffman's. Their world might be made serious by money, but this world, in the end, was made real by blood. They had crossed, in effect, more than a narrow, deep channel of Mediterranean water, a geographical boundary; they had travelled from one reality to another, just as the young soldiers did who took the dismal night ferry from Liverpool to Belfast. Sneiger, with his affected arrogance, was as ignorant of this as they, on their first tours, might be, and Davis, exchanging bitter glances with the others, chose to travel in the second vehicle. He wanted, more than anything else now, to think, to prepare, to remember everything. The photographs and plans of the bank passed slowly through his mind, as if he were seeing them again through a view finder. But he could imagine that, in the forward bus, Sneiger was already bullying them into song or distributing sandwiches or simply taking names.

The buses, having left the fields, soon found the deserted coastal road that joined Beirut to the northern towns of Jelail and Tripoli before passing into Syria and on through, eventually, to Turkey. There was another way out of Beirut, eastwards, towards the Syrian capital of Damascus or 'Esh Sham'. Davis had been careful to consider the possibilities, just as Edwards, beside him, was considering the rich fertile landscape, and the pleasant prospect of the wide gentle bay revealed by the rather grimy window.

"Nice country," he said.

"Once," Davis replied flatly. "Not now."

They travelled for two hours before turning east, leaving the coastal road and passing through small, poor-looking villages, the houses shuttered, the women already at work. Some of the men watched them pass, looking out from the shadows of buildings, their weathered faces empty of interest or intent. The buses slowed for the animals and the drivers, turning round, pointed vulgarly to the shabbily-dressed women bent over their work, never discriminating between old and young. Soon they were shouting at obstructions, swerving around them and clouding the air with a thick pelt of dust.

Eventually the convoy came to a halt, in the centre of a slightly more substantial community — there were brick houses, cultivated gardens and tree-lined avenues. Sneiger promptly ushered the mercenaries to a house, large but dilapidated, with broken shutters and rusted pieces of ironmongery strewn about the yard. The house, which at first appeared deserted, rusticated by neglect, turned out to be full of young, smiling Arabs (they would have passed for boys), whose sleeping bags and cooking utensils were everywhere in the featureless, furnitureless rooms. Most of them carried guns — FNs as well as AKs — treating them with the confident disregard of guerrillas everywhere. And, indeed, the drab house itself turned out to be nothing short of an arsenal. As they were marched eagerly from room to room by their inquisitive, attentive hosts, the mercenaries saw weapons of every description stacked against the walls, together with rows of heavy wooden crates and loose piles of shell cases. Sunlight, streaming through the broken wooden slats against the windows, illuminated careless rows of Armalites, Kalashnikovs, Mausers, Brownings, FNs, Uzis and Berrettas. Some of these weapons, on inspection, looked new and unused, others had evidently been acquired from the other side, especially the Russian and Czech guns. Davis also noticed three cartons made of thin aluminium foil which Christie identified as containing anti-tank rockets, and, in a room at the back of the house, a small, crudely-painted miniature of the Virgin Mary tacked to a wall, just above a rack of AKs. It looked rather out of place among all the hardware.

Sneiger, as ever attempting to preside over the arrangements, encouraged the mercenaries to take what they wanted from the collection. Crofts and Duncan, the SAS men, immediately expressed a preference for Kalashnikovs. Davis disagreed. For a start, he considered the FN to be a superior weapon. Produced by the Fabrique National, a Belgium company from which it took its name, the FN, used by, among others, the security forces in Rhodesia, had a special place in his affections. Though heavier and more cumbersome than nearly all its contemporaries, with a slower firing rate, its stopping power gave it a crucial advantage. The combination of a high muzzle velocity and a longer, heavier bullet gave it superior range and power. It was certainly highly effective by any standards, producing a kill from almost any hit to the head or torso. Davis had also, in the past, had the opportunity to observe from close quarters its ability to punch holes in the steel of armoured cars' bodywork.

Christie agreed with the choice, adding that they should all, for reasons of easy identification, be equipped with the same weapons. In the potentially chaotic circumstances of street fighting, the heavy thump of the FN would distinguish the mercenaries from opponents who would most probably be using Kalashnikovs and AKs.

The point won (though Crofts, perversely, also took a Browning machine gun), Davis led the men through to another room where they collected ammunition, spare magazines, hand grenades and cleaning kits, and from the aluminium cartons eight rockets. These they carried to a nearby house, their quarters until the expected arrival of Tippett from Cyprus, a barely furnished and modest brick building that must, at one time, have been a quiet family home, for there were still a few small, domestic artefacts scattered around the empty rooms, broken or abandoned by the hurriedly departing occupiers. Probably they had been Moslems, forced to leave by the bigotries of war, Davis concluded after a cursory survey.

The mercenaries settled down in one of the larger downstairs rooms, unpacking their few possessions, some of them conscientiously inspecting their newly-acquired guns, stripping and cleaning them, others resorting to the pile of magazines supplied by Christie. After a while two young Arabs appeared with a meal of bread and burnt lamb which the men, hungry after hours of travel, devoured readily, washing the scorched meat down with coffee brewed over one of their own camping stoves.

After that, Davis and Edwards went to fetch the old Bedford three-ton truck that Makmoud, before leaving for Cyprus, had found for their use. They parked it out of sight, behind the house, where the Arabs had adapted a lean-to, tin-roofed, flimsy but at least fairly spacious shed as a temporary workshop, equipping it as best they could with the cutting gear and materials Davis had requested through Hoffman. Much of it had clearly been hastily extemporised; some of the steel had obviously been stripped from other vehicles, their steering columns, seats and tyres also being in evidence. Odd bits of metal, some corroded by age, engine parts, hefty pieces of angle iron, had all been collected and thrown to the back of the shed with apparently careless indifference. The tarnished metal gleamed dully under the single naked light.

The two men examined the materials methodically, sorting out the useful bits and pieces, separating them from the rest.

"Well," Edwards said, wiping his hands, "what do you think?"

Davis remembered, without affection, some of the rudimentary Angolan equipment.

"It's good enough. No more than . . . ten hours work."

Edwards groaned audibly.

"Don't complain!" Davis retorted sharply. "This fucking thing might save your life. I'm not doing it for fun, you know."

"But ten hours!"

"Probably longer. I didn't want to worry you. Just look at this shit!"

Edwards looked, and shrugged.

"Where do we start?" he said.

They started by laboriously cutting out the protective steel plates designed to cover the entire outer shell of the vehicle. That operation alone took them over ten long hours and well into the night, and when they finally took a break, just before dawn, their hands bore the evidence of their crude physical labours, cut and blistered from the constant abrasions of metal against flesh.

Still, four hours later they were back at work, removing the tubular bars from the truck's superstructure and replacing the whole with a lower frame of angle iron. Then they welded the steel plates on to the frame in an irregular, overlapping pattern, leaving narrow slits in the sides as well as round the edges of the roof to facilitate firing in all directions. The protective pattern of plates was repeated over the cab itself.

The windscreen was replaced with two thin sheets of steel with more openings near the top, to which Davis added a number of smaller, heavier plates, welding them at odd angles but leaving reciprocal apertures that allowed the driver clear if limited vision.

Among the junk in the workshop Edwards had found several old and worn ball joints from the steering systems of various cars and lorries. These were welded to more angle iron, and then in turn welded across four square holes cut out at each corner of the roof. The joints, reinforced by crudely constructed clamps, formed mountings for Uzi submachine guns. Although the guns, by virtue of their position, could only be fired indiscriminately, the sponsons enabled them to be loaded, cocked and fired with nothing but the gunner's hand being visible. And since they would be able to spray bullets rapidly over a wide area this arrangement, makeshift as it was, appeared adequate.

Finally, at the back of the truck — now nick-named "Aggie" by Edwards — Davis welded a tailgate, more plates, and a mounting for one of the machine guns. Four skirts, made out of lighter plate, covered and protected the wheels, and yet another the engine compartment.

At last it was finished.

"Looks like a sodding armadillo," Johnson remarked wryly,

inspecting the curious vehicle that might also have passed, with its thick and dull metal scales, for a First World War tank without tread or barrel.

But Davis himself, despite the sarcastic comments, was reasonably satisfied. The suspension was down perceptibly and, after test-driving it, he found the truck to be not only slower, as expected, but clumsier and less responsive, pulling constantly and irritatingly to the right, though there was little that could now be done to redress the balance. On the other hand, and somewhat more importantly, Aggie proved an effective shield, stopping all the Kalashnakov bullets fired at its flanks (the mercenaries had lined up as though for a firing squad), and some of the heavier FN rounds which riccocheted away from the irregular plates.

Sneiger, from a safe distance, watched the iron truck lumber clumsily round the open field and listened to the clatter of the guns, the whine of bullets flattened on contact and harmlessly deflected. He felt out of place, nervously aware of his precarious vulnerability, and of the necessity of travelling the next day into the ruined and mutinous city to the south. He was well aware of the mercenaries' mistrust, which had begun to seem more like antagonism. He felt equally unsure of the Arabs, whose moods were fickle and volatile. The mercenaries' response had been to place a guard outside their sleeping quarters, reinforcing a mutual suspicion that augured badly for the approaching mission. Sneiger's own attempts to allay it, on both sides, had proved fruitless, leaving him moreover out in the cold. It was hardly a situation he relished, nor was it one he had particularly envisaged. Theoretically, at least, he was to have enjoyed the close co-operation of the Christian forces; in fact, they appeared not to discriminate, in their increasingly abrasive manner, between the mercenaries and himself. He could only trust to the expectation that Chamoun's man, Makmoud, would prove a better, more willing and amicable ally.

He was not to be disappointed. An hour later, the last of daylight, saw the arrival of both Makmoud and Tippett, together with the jars of explosives. Sneiger wasted no time in drawing the Lebanese away to one side, and found him well-prepared and informative, though rather aggrieved at the behaviour of the mercenary in Cyprus. They discussed the operation carefully, rehearsing each step, including the final deployment of the Phalangists inside the bank.

"You must keep your men away from the ground floor and the vault," Sneiger emphasised. "We don't want to alert anyone . . . prematurely. Right?"

"Yes," Makmoud said slowly. "But what is prem—?"

"Too soon," snapped the American. "Do you understand? They musn't get suspicious of you. I'll tell you when to move, by radio, but before that you've got to keep out of sight."

"Yes," Makmoud said. "I understand."

"Good. Then, when I give the signal, you'll have something like three minutes to complete the . . . you know?"

"My men will be ready. It's nothing," and Makmoud gestured dismissively.

"Don't underestimate them."

The Lebanese fell silent for a moment, his face set, as if he was taking the warning to heart. Instead he concluded grimly,

"It is always us who have been underestimated, Mr Sneiger."

Sneiger walked away, finding Davis and Tippett re-examining the photographs of the vault door inside the house. Outside, in the thick darkness, he had passed another mercenary cradling his FN who had simply nodded, impassively, as if he had been a stranger.

Davis was less truculent, but equally formal.

"When's the final briefing?" he wanted to know.

Sneiger nodded. "That's what I've come about. Can you get everyone in here, right now?"

Tippett left the room to find the others, and Sneiger automatically drew the handkerchief from his pocket and dabbed at his brow.

"I think we ought to do something to calm people down," he told Davis quietly.

"I'm perfectly calm," Davis replied.

"You know what I mean! I can tell that some of the men are edgy, that's all."

Davis lit a cigarette.

"They don't like the way the Arabs are behaving," he said. "And neither do I. I thought we were doing them a favour."

"You are. I guess some people don't like having to ask for one. Anyway," Sneiger added, "I've seen to it. There won't be any trouble."

Suppressing a smile, Davis, contemptuous of the other's power to organise the gun-happy Phalangists, nodded in feigned tacit agreement. Then, turning away, he watched the men assembling in the room that had already begun to smell of their collective sweat. He assessed them: Edwards cheerfully cleaning his nails, telling a joke, snorting with sudden laughter; Christie, small and furtive and uneasy, scuffing his boots on the wooden floor, his eyes darting about from one face to another, seeking something, some consolation or comfort; Tippett, just arrived, lazily leaning against a wall, bored and obviously thinking about something else, smoking, indifferent, half-amused, his eyes heavy-lidded and occasionally closing; the two SAS, Crofts and Duncan, both tall, athletic, one blond the other dark, slightly fuller of face and now bearded, both keen, alert, attentive, disciplined. Davis neither liked nor disliked them, though their background had set them apart from the rest. So far he had not had much of an opportunity to talk to either, but at least he had had time to take notes, noticing their technical proficiencies, their easy accuracy with assorted weapons. Undoubtedly they were good professionals, in theory, and yet he also had a reassuring sense, nothing more than instinct, that pleasantly-mannered though they were they were mentally tougher than others of their kind. Of course there was only one kind of proof of that inner quality, that iron in the soul, that ability to endure beyond hope and despair, but even so Davis had learned over the years to trust his instincts. Experience had sharpened them considerably. He looked them over again, reaffirming his judgement. They were okay. They would do. Christie had been right. But he hoped to God they weren't already in the man's pocket.

Johnson was called in from outside, entering quietly and unobtrusively and without comment. His expression betrayed nothing, neither interest nor enthusiasm, and he went to stand by himself against a far wall. True to form he had not fraternised, had kept his distance and even practised alone, but then much more frequently than the other mercenaries. Candid and not unfriendly when approached, Johnson was nevertheless the kind whose reticence and reserve were automatically respected. It was not a grudging admiration, and there was no false pride in Johnson's invariable detachment. He simply did not go out of his way to be popular, and perhaps it was this, together with his hard consistency, which ironically made him so.

"This is your final briefing," Davis began abruptly. "You'd better listen. Tomorrow we're going in, and then it'll be too late to ask questions." He turned to Sneiger, cleared his throat noisily, glanced around the room and stepped forward.

"Tomorrow afternoon, towards dusk, Christian militia will attack five Moslem-held positions in the city. Three of these attacks will be diversionary — but the other two sectors will be taken. And from there, Christian artillery will be able to direct fire into one of the large PLO camps to the south of Beirut.

"Apart from the incidental damage this will cause it will also have the effect of drawing Moslem forces away from the banking area, and as soon as that happens we'll go in behind them." Sneiger paused, mopping his brow. "Their job will be to clear away the roadblocks inside the city and allow us clear access to the bank. Once we're there, however, most of them will move out and establish a perimeter, preventing an immediate counter-attack. Now, I'm told that the perimeter can be held for a maximum of ten hours; that's a *maximum* of ten hours. After, irrespective of anything else, and whether or not you've completed your part of the job, they'll have to pull out."

Sneiger paused again, but could tell nothing from the

expression on the men's faces. He went on hurriedly.

"If everything goes according to plan we'll be leaving here around four in the morning, coincident with the second wave of shelling. The Christians will precede you into the bank itself, establishing positions on the upstairs floors. The ground floor will be left to you. The next job, naturally, will be getting that fucking vault door open, and when that's done I'll hand over the keys to the safety deposit section and the safeboxes."

"Why don't you hand them over now?" Tippett asked brusquely.

Sneiger shook his head.

"Because you don't need them now." He sounded almost belligerent, and the sound pleased him. "Your task is simple; and you'll be chaperoned there and back. There's no need for you to be concerned with any of the details. Is that understood?"

Tippett looked quickly across at Davis, who inclined his head slightly. There was little point in taxing the American now. They were committed — though something in that brief, slight gesture also counselled patience. There would be time, Davis knew, to sort out the man, and every reason to. But for the moment they would let him be, allow him the luxury of this charade, the false glamour of his authority.

As if to dispense it further, Sneiger continued,

"Tomorrow morning I'll be handing out your arm bands. The Lebanese will be wearing them too, for identification . . ." he caught Davis's quizzical look. "It's a sensible precaution."

"Sure," replied the other. "I always wear one."

The irony wasn't lost.

"Well, on this occasion you will. Now, are there any more questions?"

There weren't, and Sneiger broke up the meeting. After he had left the room Davis went across the floor to speak to Johnson.

"Well?"

"Well what?" Johnson said.

86

"What do you think?"

"I don't," Johnson smiled briefly. "I don't think. People who think too much never do anything. Anyway, I'm going to let you do the thinking for me, Davis. All right?"

Davis watched the tall mercenary stride slowly across to the door, noticing the unconscious arrogance of his walk. "You shit," he said quietly. "You shit." But there was no malice in the word.

6

The whole of the next long, sunlit day was spent checking ammunition in spare magazines, putting fresh water in spare canteens, listlessly, compulsively cleaning the mechanism of weapons that were already clean. The hours were whittled away in restless anticipation. Then, as the shadows began to lengthen and the air cooled, faces turned expectantly towards the invisible city away to the south, and the pantomime of preparation was gradually abandoned. The elderly Arab who brought goat's cheese, hummus and bread over at each mealtime came and went without anybody really noticing. Outside the huts and along the roadside the Phalangists appeared, squatting on their haunches in small clusters, talking quietly, their voices like the insistent murmur of summer insects. Together they watched the failing sun sink finally below the line of distant green hills, and the sky turn from a light, clear blue to a delicate, transluscent mauve, flecked with pink.

They waited. Time seemed to pass by empty-handed as the shadows closed in around them, like a curtain drawn over an open window. Then, from behind it, surprising them despite their expectations, came the first vivid, phosphorescent orange and crimson flashes, followed by the rolling thunder and reverberations — like a sudden, violent tropical storm. Although out of sight, the guns and rockets lit up the Arabian sky like an artificial sunset, glowing with rich colours that bled into one another before melting away. Occasionally a high white flare, bursting open like shrapnel, momentarily illuminated an eerie, unreal landscape, and all the while the night air was full of the long staccato chatter of automatic gunfire. After a time, despite the confusion of sounds, they could distinguish between the light quick clatter of the Kalashnikovs, over to the right, and the heavier, more solid bangs of the FNs, each side answering the other in the ritual exchange of war.

The barrage lasted three hours. During all that time, however, none of the watchers had stopped to turn away and talk, or take their eyes away from the brilliant spectacle, as fascinating as a firework display or an electric storm. But, suddenly, except for a faint, distant crackle, a solitary, luminous, dying flare, it ceased. The quiet darkness smothered them again, strange in its ordinariness, like the still, abrupt moment at the end of a film, before the house lights go on.

Still the mercenaries had to wait, to occupy the time before the commencement of the second and final barrage, if it came. All of them had long ago abandoned any notion of sleeping. A brew of coffee at two thirty had helped to push the cold night's chill away, but now nothing could mitigate its severity, keep them from shivering. Davis, exercising the cramped muscles in his legs, walked back to the house and returned with a bundle of thin, threadbare blankets, distributing them to the men on the ground. He noticed that some of the Arabs had already kindled fires, for the small flames flickered in the darkness creating a strange, ghostly scene, as spectral figures passed beyond the warm circle of firelight.

At four o'clock the guns, having clearly gained their new positions, opened up again and the sky began to burn for the second time. At almost the same moment, further up the road, the engine of the first minibus coughed abruptly to life, its headlights blazing, followed by the second. Without a word the seven mercenaries climbed into "Aggie" and Davis, at the wheel, swung the Bedford onto the road and brought it up behind the convoy. Their own lights illuminated the curious, almost bizarre spectacle of traditional kef-i-yah headdresses and gun barrels, these latter protruding from nearly every window of the nearest bus. But then, as the vehicles accelerated away, the barbed vision was lost to sight, and since Davis was forced to drive slowly because of the box of grease balanced across Tippett's knees, it wasn't long before even the tail lights of the bus had faded into the darkness.

Davis informed the others.

"So much for a fucking convoy," Edwards muttered. "What are the bastards playing at?" He rubbed his unshaved jaw reflectively.

Christie, peering anxiously through the narrow slit in the windscreen, looked at Davis and fumbled for a cigarette.

"They'll wait for us?" He said it, uneasily, as a question.

Davis shrugged.

"I've no idea. Just watch the road, will you?"

The old truck bounced and rattled along the uneven surface, responding clumsily to Davis's ministrations, slithering as it turned. Somehow he kept it glued to the road and, after a few miles, to either side they could see the first drab outskirts of the city, the houses picked out in the beam of the headlights, gradually assuming a harder shape as the first fingers of pale grey light touched the horizon. Dawn was not far away. Then the road dropped down between the first set of tall, faceless apartment blocks, and curved to the left. Coming out of the steep bend slowly, Davis suddenly saw the tail end of the convoy: the minibus was stopped, its front wheels on the pavement, its lights doused. Davis pulled Aggie in behind it, under the shelter of some trees, and was conscious as he did so of the slight bustle of activity behind him, of the cocking of weapons, the movement of faces towards the thin, blind apertures. He experienced too the first real surge of adrenalin and caught, briefly and accidentally, a glimpse of Christie's prematurely anxious face reflected grimly in the mirror.

Sneiger appeared at the side of the truck and spoke quietly through the opening where the driver's window used to be.

"We're held up about half a kilometre down the road. Some kind of armoured vehicle, with a machine gun. I guess they're having some problems with it."

"I don't hear anything," replied Davis sharply, scanning the

90

unlit street. Perhaps the Phalangists herded into the forward bus had simply become jittery, had lost their nerve and paniched. It wasn't long, however, before the unmistakable sound of the Kalashnikovs was followed by the heavier, resonant thump of a large-calibre machine gun. Davis listened to the exchange for a moment, silently cursing the delay, then opened the door and stepped out, watching a few remote lights flicker on behind apartment windows high above them. He removed the two rockets from beneath the front seat of the cab and called for Tippett and Edwards to join him on the ground.

Then Makmoud bustled over. He was grinning and seemed not in the least disconcerted.

"Murabitoun," he said. "Moslem left. Gangsters."

"So what's the problem?"

"Many soldiers," the Lebanese responded.

"How many?"

"Six — or ten."

Davis reflected that there were two full busloads of Christian soldiers, but said nothing.

"Usually," Sneiger interrupted, "there's no more than two or three kids manning those blocks. Teenagers with pistols in their back pockets."

"Never underestimate an armed and angry teenager," Davis snapped.

He gave Edwards one of the rockets and the three mercenaries, skirting the vulnerable buses, walked forward cautiously. They found individual Phalangists crouching in the shelter of ruined doorways, directing occasional bursts of fire at the Murabitouns' crude barricade. Two bodies lay, face down in the road, evidence of an initial clumsy rush-attack.

The real obstacle, however, was not the assembly of tin-drums and planks but a truck, broadside behind it, on the deck of which the Moslems had erected a sponson holding a thirty calibre machine gun. The gunner, flush from his early success, was now successfully pinning down the rest of the uneasy squad. Beside him, so far as the mercenaries could ascertain,

91

there were only two other men, and one of them appeared to be wounded.

Nevertheless there was little point in prolonging the engagement and risking the arrival of fresh defenders. They would have to squander part of their insurance: the rockets.

The first, fired from Edward's shoulder, caught the back of the truck. The second, following directly, struck the cab. The vehicle and machine gunner disappeared in a cloud of dust and bits of flying human and machine debris. From the centre of this manmade malestrom came the muted sound of a single shot — then silence.

There seemed little possibility of anyone else surviving the twin blasts, but to make absolutely certain Tippett, further ahead than the other two, stepped out and sprayed the burning truck with his FN — a controlled but devastating splatter of bullets.

There was no response, and suddenly the street was full of Christian soldiers, some of them dismantling the barrier, others relishing the sight of the decapitated gunner and the wreckage. Davis left them to it and went back to Aggie, indicating to the bus drivers that it was time to move on.

The journey continued slowly, the convoy continually harrassed by solitary snipers or groups of young soldiers in camouflage fatigues who appeared to fire indiscriminately upon anyone with the temerity to move around the streets unannounced. It was probable, Davis thought, that each group belonged to one or another of the many factions which were all loosely described as the Moslem left. Yet it was equally likely that, in furtherance of some petty, internecine rivalry, they believed themselves to be attacking their own kind. No-one, however, made any sustained effort to prevent their passage and as the suburbs gave way to the city proper they had managed to avoid any further roadblocks — though as everyone knew this had more to do with luck than foresight. In Beirut, new barricades went up almost every night, assembled by one party or another determined to claim fresh territory. They came down just as quickly — but usually not before some luckless motorist had been caught in the trap and, equally usually, killed without question. It was true that, each evening, a certain radio announcer would indicate the safe roads, but even then they might not remain safe for more than a few hours. So, for Davis, this was almost the most vulnerable part of the entire enterprise. They had no way of knowing what lay ahead, around the next corner, at the end of the next street.

He had heard, from Hoffman and from others, what the years of fighting had done to Beirut — but nothing could really have prepared him or his colleagues for this first sight of the devastated city. They were now surrounded by the towering apartment blocks that had once housed a thriving, affluent population. Not one seemed to have escaped the brutal scars of war. The façades had been pitted by machine gun fire, lumps of masonry had been wrenched away and fallen into the streets below, and everywhere huge black soot stains rose up, like bruises, from smashed windows that looked out of empty, fire-gutted rooms.

Many of the buildings were uninhabitable, so profound was the damage. In others, behind closed shutters, a certain kind of life was visible as people who could not or would not move away clung miserably but tenaciously to what was left, trying to salvage what they could from the carnage. London might have looked a little similar, Davis thought, after the bombers had visited it.

With all the rubble, the glass and cement, the burnt-out cars and trucks, he had some difficulty keeping Aggie close to the shelter of the kerb. Whenever he was forced out nearer the middle of the road their presence was invariably greeted with a burst of gunfire from a concealed gunman, the bullets rattling and whining against the roof and sides of the armoured car. Its occupants did their best to return the fire, opening up the Uzi on the roof in an optimistic attempt to catch a luckless sniper. Occasionally they caught glimpses from the narrow apertures of men in striped headcloths peering down from a roof or around the corner of a building, and sometimes they were forced to stop to allow the Phalangists to pick off nearer targets.

At last they saw a building that had once, in better days, housed a small bank, though now its windows were boarded up and its roof was missing. They had arrived at the banking centre and a mere twenty metres ahead, where the road opened out into a small square, there was the object of their journey, the American Bank. They recognised it at once, but were simultaneously aware of heavy fighting going on in the adjoining buildings as the Phalangists, disgorged by the buses, ran across the square and lobbed hand grenades through the lower windows. At first it wasn't clear how many armed elements were inside, returning fire. There were certainly no signs of life at the upper windows, and as fire started to lick through the rooms it became more and more evident that the Phalangists were once again overplaying their hand. Then, one by one, men with guns began to appear on the roof, driven up by the flames. Crofts and Duncan climbed out onto the tailgate of Aggie and meticulously began to pick them off, one by one. Rather than lie down to escape the murderously accurate sniping the men on the roof, trapped by the blaze below them, seemed confused and simply remained where they were like so many wooden targets in a booth. When one went down, another took his place and it even seemed to Davis, watching from below and the protection of Aggie's cab, that one or two actually jumped of their own volition, crumpling up like rag dolls the second they hit the pavement below, the sound of it all hidden by the continuous noise of battle, the shouts, the shattering of glass.

Yet at least one man must have kept his head, if only for a moment, because Crofts was suddenly knocked off his stance on the tailgate by a bullet that creased him alongside his ear. He fell backwards and sideways into the roadway where a second round hit him in the pit of the stomach and blew him away as easily as an autumn leaf. Under covering fire that streamed haphazardly out of the Uzis Duncan leapt down and began to drag the wounded man back to the safety of the Iron

Maiden. Croft's violent contortions, however, made any movement difficult and after struggling for a long thirty seconds, Duncan struck him hard.

Once under the tailgate of the Bedford, after a morphine injection, the bloody opening that used to be the man's stomach was stuffed crudely with field dressings and then bound. Davis wondered what was going through Christie's mind as he watched the hopeless and messy operation, but Christie remained silent throughout it, only occasionally looking down as the fast dying man, his life blood pouring out, muttered some feeble, incomprehensible phrase that was perhaps a desperate prayer to be released from his incurable agony.

Looking towards the bank, Davis saw the familiar figure of the Phalangist leader Makmoud waving the Brits over. The stocky man from Camberley started the truck's engine and drove the Bedford into the square, turned to the right and followed the road around the centre-piece of the small quadrangle.

The bank lay almost directly opposite the road they had taken into the square extending from its right-hand corner almost to its centre, an imposing frontage of nearly two hundred feet. The view of the exit road was obstructed by a statue and a fountain, which took up most of the space in the centre of the square. The uniform height of the buildings surrounding that road shut out most of the strong sunlight to give an air of gloom. In any other circumstances the road would be a shaded, cool haven, but to Davis it represented anything but a haven. Swinging the truck around, he stopped, selected reverse gear and, with Makmoud's aid, reversed into the gaping hole that had once been an expensive façade. The wheels bumped over the bodies of the dead Moslem gunmen, hapless victims of a plot that had little to do with their religious war. Davis ran the truck back into the darkened interior until the tailgate was a few feet from the long mahogany counter. He switched off the motor.

At last Tippett was able to take the box of grease off his knees and stretch his long legs.

"We made it," he murmured. And, except for the prone figure of Crofts, on the floor by their feet, they had. So far.

7

Dr George Habash, leader of the Popular Front for the Libera-
tion of Palestine, was very angry. As usual, his anger was
hidden behind the mask of chilled calculated reserve he always
presented to the world — but nevertheless his closest aides
could detect it, and knew better than to ask its cause. Most of
them in any case, were well aware of the cause, for Habash had
just returned from one of his periodic meetings with Arafat,
overall leader of the P.L.O. but a man with whom Habash
often disagreed. For a start Habash was a Marxist and Arafat,
despite the colour of this rhetoric, had no real political ideo-
logy, though a great many political ambitions. Habash considered him, at best, an opportunist with a flair for drawing
people to the cause. He had great personal presence, like
Castro, and used that fact to win over the leaders of the other
seven independent guerrilla groups fighting for Palestinian
freedom. The danger for Habash was that at any moment
Arafat might betray the confidence they had all placed in his
leadership, just to appear at the United Nations as an equal of
any elected President, and as the saviour of the Palestinians
now crowded in their miserable shanty-towns. To appear so he
might be forced to accept political compromises in the name of
judicial statesmanship. For Habash, on the other hand, there
could be no compromises.

Beyond that fundamental distinction between the two men,
however, lay many others of a more practical nature. They
often disagreed about short-term objectives, about guerrilla
tactics, about the ways of attracting the world's attention to the

plight of the refugees. Arafat, characteristically, often changed his mind over these questions. Sometimes he would advocate dramatic and violent solutions, at other times he would counsel moderation, arguing that hi-jacking and slaughter of innocents did as much harm as good, for while they attracted attention they lost sympathy. World sympathy, he insisted, was one of the P.L.O.'s primary weapons: without it there was little chance of the United Nations or anyone else bringing necessary pressure to bear on Israel to relinquish some of its stolen lands.

Habash, on the whole, thought differently — was more inclined to follow the path set out by Lenin in his great pamphlets on the seizure of power in Russia. He believed that what the United Nations wanted more than anything was to forget the issue, and that the only real resolution would come about by force, from the letting of blood from inside. There were, after all, not one but many historical precedents. He was also strongly in favour of political assassinations. Individuals were always more vulnerable than states and nothing caused more panic than a judicious murder, or seemed to have such an effect in comparison to the effort required to carry it out.

Today, as on many previous occasions, this had been the actual cause of his disagreement with Arafat. Arafat had wanted to prevent any further assassinations, at least for the time being. He had argued that, over the last year, their cumulative effect had been insignificant and, on top of that, that there were too many groups around the world indulging in the same activity.

Who was to tell who killed who, when there were so many contradictory claims? The impact had been lost. People were beginning to accept, cynically but inevitably, such murders. They winced, shrugged their shoulders and simply forgot about them.

All the time Arafat had been speaking, patiently explaining his position, Habash had a suspicion that he was hiding something, perhaps some private agreement with a Western leader. Now, back at his headquarters, he was convinced this was so, though there was nothing he could do about it and no way he could find out. What he could do was simply to ignore Arafat's request — to go ahead with his schedule of assassinations. In the end, of course, this could mean the end of his association with the parent body of the PLO but even that didn't disturb him unduly. Again the example of Lenin proved what could be done with a smaller, more committed group.

He produced, from his desk, a single sheet of paper with a long list of names — and nothing else — typed out in three columns. He looked down the columns carefully, sometimes scribbling a comment beside a particular name. Then he passed the piece of paper to the man sitting opposite, leaned back and raised his eyebrows quizzically. He even smiled faintly, for having made his decision he was already feeling more composed.

The man repeated the exercise, making his own comments.

"We agree, then," Habash said, examining the paper again. "It shouldn't be anyone too important — not this time. Arafat would make trouble. It has to be someone closely connected to our . . . problems. Yes?"

The other man nodded.

"Someone whose death would mean more to those in power, those who organize against us, those who support Israel. There would be no public outcry — just a meeting, an urgent meeting between a few close colleagues. They would know. It would be a symbol."

"That leaves the three Americans."

"Yes. So. Who do you favour?"

"Samuel. We should hit Samuel."

Habash, leaning forward again, frowned with obvious disapproval.

"You miss my point," he said mildly. "Samuel is . . . too important. Who else?"

"There's only one."

"Who? I'm asking you to tell me."

"Hoffman."

"Exactly." The smile, more radiant, returned. "There is no

one else. We know about Hoffman's crimes, his connections in Israel, his feelings about us. There will always be others to replace him of course . . ." He dismissed the argument with a wave of his hand. ". . . but until now they've believed them all safe. And why? Because they're not important enough. Just cogs. But remove a cog and for a while the machine falters, questions are asked. That's why Hoffman has to be . . . a victim."

"I'll see to it," the other man said, and rose to his feet. "We have a file. He won't be hard to find."

"And when you find him, make sure."

The man nodded his head.

"Of course," he said.

8

The mercenaries — except Duncan who was left to guard
Aggie, cover the front of the bank and the square beyond —
followed the Phalangists into the building and then split up
according to a prearranged plan. Johnson went to the rear of
the building which looked out upon a wide, empty road. Both
he and Duncan were given radios. Davis and Tippett, with
Sneiger carrying the grease, went immediately down the stairs
to the vault while the remaining two, ostensibly searching the
other floors for undiscovered Moslem gunmen, were actually
examining the positioning of the Christians. If there had been
any Palestinians in the building they certainly left no
evidence. The three bodies on the deserted second floor had
clearly been dead for a considerable time since their bodies,
pushed against the wall, were already bloated and beginning to
decompose. The stench permeated the area around them,
despite the broken windows, attracting thousands of blue and
bloated flies which feasted in lazy droves.

The mercenaries looked at the dead men dispassionately,
then moved on, ascertaining that the Christians, however
many of them there were, had left the first and second floors
unattended and assembled on the third. They saw at least two
of them, with machine guns, situated at the head of a flight of
stairs and it seemed likely that the rest were either behind
them, with Makmoud, or up on the roof. However, on the
identical but seriously damaged staircase at the other end of
the building they found another three gunmen. Curiously, for
men supposed to be guarding against assault from outside,

they had set up a machine gun amongst the twisted steel and concrete rubble that looked down upon the second floor. They recognised the mercenaries with brief nods, before continuing their private conversation. Leaving Edwards behind a make-shift barricade of masonary in the centre of the floor, Christie went down to tell Davis about the machine gun.

On the way he heard the first explosion; a solid, dust-raising thump identified it unmistakably. And when he arrived he found Tippett already setting the second of the "shaped" charges around the fissure in the great door which were designed to blow a small diameter hole through the thick, resistent layers of Glass, Steel and Clay.

Employing what was called the "Munro" effect, the steel-cased plastic explosive, when detonated, drove the steel, now molten, into the face of the vault door. And it was indeed possible to see the massive, multi-layered door slowly yielding under the fantastic pressure of each successive charge. After the fourth one Tippett, holding a torch to the red hot and punctured hole, declared the operation successful. The others watched with interest as he took an old inner tube for a motor-bike and began to push it through the hole, though they all noticed at once the smell of scorching, melting rubber. Tippett yanked it back sharply.

"Fuck that!"

"It's too hot," Sneiger remarked placidly, wiping his brow. "You'll have to wait till it cools."

Tippett glared at him angrily.

"It won't," he said, "not for a long time. Some of the layers in that thing are made of tungsten, set beside others that are a kind of fire clay. That means they absorb heat. Get it?"

Sneiger might have resented being treated like a child, but for the moment he said nothing, and glanced away.

"What's the point of the tube anyway?" Davis enquired.

"Look. I'm going to push it down the internal cavity where the lock mechanism is. That'll concentrate the explosion. Nothing else is going to shift this bastard."

"How long do we wait?"

Tippett shrugged.

"Can you find some water . . . a bucketful? If not, an hour, perhaps two."

"We can't wait that long."

"What can I do?"

Davis sent Christie away to look for a source of water, knowing full well there wouldn't be one and that one stupid oversight, on Tippett's part, was now jeopardizing the operation.

While he was gone, Tippett laid out a roll of light twin flex up the stairs, along the corridor, through the shattered security gate at the end and then outside, near the rear of the truck, where a curious, unexpected quiet had settled over the immediate vicinity of the bank. A few pigeons fluttered harmlessly from roof to roof, fanning grey wings against the expanse of light blue. Otherwise the only sound was that of Tippett's boots crunching over broken glass in the yard. It seemed as if Beirut, so used to having its midday siesta disturbed, had settled easily back to inconsequential sleep. Tippett, looking around, gave the thumbs up sign to Duncan, then retraced his steps.

Downstairs, as he had somehow expected, the water problem had been smartly resolved. Grinning widely, Christie presented him with a waste paper bin full of urine, freshly collected.

"Fine," he agreed, and doused the door until it was tempered enough for him to insert the tubing, and until there was a strong smell of ammonia in the air. After that, with infinite caution, he poured the thick, treacly grease down the narrow opening, and they were ready.

With everyone outside Tippett unloaded two batteries from the back of Aggie, linked them in parallel, then connected one side of the flex to the negative terminal. He glanced up briefly at Davis.

"If I believed in God I'd start to pray," he said flatly, and with that jammed the other loose end onto the positive terminal.

There was an unbelievable explosion, swelling out underground like a steel blister bursting, followed by a sudden rush of thick swirling dust along the corridor, gushing like volcanic ash out of the doorway.

"You shit!" Sneiger shouted above the noise. "You shit! You've blown the fucking place to bits."

The others, ignoring him, groped their way blindly back down the stairs, hands over mouths, blinking back scalding tears. Smoke and dust still blossomed around them, thick as fog, dispersing slowly.

At the bottom they found the great front plate of the vault door, twisted and buckled, its ten-ton weight having been tossed blithely by the force of the blast at least twenty feet. One edge was now buried in the solid concrete wall of the passageway. Climbing over it they reached what remained of the door itself. Though coughing and choking, they felt momentarily elated: the explosion had literally split the thing into two separate halves, removing one half completely and leaving the other bent backwards in the frame like an opened, serated tincan lid — only this lid still had seven two-inch steel bars holding it into the frame. The remaining bars had given way, or been snapped like twigs, but the gap between them, though giving a view of the strongroom, was too small to allow access.

Sneiger, still making a pretence of overseeing matters, wrung his hands in disappointment, until Tippett assured him gruffly that another charge would complete the job. Then, apparently satisfied, he retreated back along the corridor and picked up a radio. Davis, watching him carefully despite the deliberately turned back, assumed that he must be talking to Makmoud on the roof. He nudged Edwards who followed his gaze and nodded. Edward's expression, meeting his, betrayed the contempt they shared for the exotic, transparent American . . . but that quick, familiar nod also signified something else, the confirmation of an arrangement made days before, in the uncertain hours when the English mercenaries had discussed Hoffman's real intentions. Then they had merely been speculating; now the certainties were everywhere around them. It was just a question of timing.

Before detonating the final charge, Davis had contacted Edwards on the radio. Now he looked across to Tippett, who'd listened to the conversation so far. Tippett casually glanced around at his explosive preparations before giving Davis a positive nod, and Davis pressed his transmit butto.

"Just two more bangs, Mike — just two more bangs." Edwards replied that he'd heard him the first time, and then the four mercenaries holding walkie-talkie radios took the slim blue sets out of their leather holders, unscrewed the large chrome nut on the side and removed the back of the set. They unscrewed the grey crystals and replaced them with the mauve ones thus changing the receiving and transmitting frequency. This prearranged plan was a product of the mass of mistrust, felt initially by Davis since he first met Hoffman in London, and felt more keenly by the other two principle mercenaries during the short stay in the village prior to their journey actually into Beirut. Sneiger noticed Davis changing the crystal and seemed to be on the point of protesting, but changed his mind and said nothing. In any case, they were all obliged to move out of the basement area to avoid the blast of the final explosion. At the head of the staircase, the American spoke rapidly into his radio set in Arabic. Davis and Tippett made a pretence of checking the wire down into the vault area to give them time for a quick conflab, plus a quick message to the pair of Brits on the upper level of the building. It was there Davis learnt that four of the Phalangists had just passed Edwards and were on their way to meet with Sneiger at the top of the stairs. Davis muttered another message into the transmitter and he had his companion made their way back to where the American had been: Tippett let the final blast rip, and in a tumult of smoke and flying masonry the rest of the giant vault door was ripped from its frame and tossed to one side, like a discarded toy. The vault was wide open . . .

9

Makmoud listened to Sneiger's excited voice over the radio. Sneiger told him that Tippett was laying the last two charges and that the vault would be open in an hour. Then he said to come down and also that there were only three mercenaries in the vault, he didn't know where the others were. Makmoud could see one of them below him, using a mirror, crouching behind some stones, but he didn't say this because he thought Sneiger was a fool to talk so openly on the radio when others could be listening. He told Sneiger instead that his men were ready to cover the mercenaries when they started to load the funny-looking truck. Sneiger said good, that was fine, just be ready.

Afterwards Makmoud thought that, for some reason, the American was lying: how could it take an hour to open the vault if Tippett was already placing the last charges? Perhaps, he thought, Sneiger wanted time to go into the vault himself and stuff his pockets full of jewels. Sneiger looked just like that: greedy and selfish. Makmoud thought all Americans were probably like that, petty criminals, gangsters, without honour. He wanted very much to kill Sneiger — but instead he had to kill the Englishmen, even Tippett, whom he respected a little. Perhaps there would be an opportunity. He could make it look like an accident or, even better, make it look like the English had murdered him. The idea pleased Makmoud and he laughed.

Then he told the others, quietly, that they should wait. He could see they were becoming restless, fingering their guns,

106

complaining . . . but he despised impatience. Most of them anyway were no more than children: street gunmen. They liked going round in gangs, picking on innocent people walking by themselves, fooling with them, burning their hands, kicking their genitals, shooting them in the arms or legs or feet for fun. When they were bored they shot them in the head and left them. Few of these young boys had ever put themselves in danger. Few of them cared who they murdered. Sometimes they didn't even bother to find out whether a woman was a Christian or a Moslem, before they raped her and cut her throat. They would even pretend not to notice a cross — though they were wise enough to remove it afterwards, in case someone responsible found out what they were up to and punished them. Makmoud often spat at them for their mischief, but now he just had to sit back and watch them pace up and down the empty floor, grumbling.

There were twelve left, which meant six killed or badly wounded: two at the roadblock and the rest in the burning building. Outside he had posted few guards, just beyond the bank, with radios. But something, he noticed, had gone wrong with the radios, because he could no longer hear the mercenaries talking to one another. Before Sneiger's call he could hear everything — now just his own men. He didn't believe that the others had suddenly stopped communicating. No, it was something else. They were clever. It was stupid to think, as Sneiger seemed to, that they believed everything. Probably already they were suspicious. That meant they were prepared. And what if they had only six men? Six men like this were better than an army like his. They knew how to fight. They didn't scuttle away under the nearest stone when the odds were against them. After all, the odds were always against them.

Makmoud knew that his best chance was to pretend, to take some of his men with him down to the vault and isolate the two mercenaries there . . . With Davis and Tippett out of the way . . .

The Arab leader took three others with him and carefully

107

made his way past the two Englishmen on the first floor. As he walked past them he knew that Sneiger had misjudged, that the British were aware. He looked into their eyes and saw death covered by restraint, saw thin smiles covering hate. They knew. He met the American on the stairs, below Edwards, as the final charge blew. They all fell in a heap as the building shook for the last time, and then talked quickly and quietly as the great belch of dust resettled itself.

Meeting Tippett at the top of the staircase that led to the vault, Sneiger asked:

"Well, have you done it this time?"

"Don't know till we go down and have a look," replied the explosives expert. Tippett led the party down into the swirling, dust-filled blackness that was the vault. Holding the torch, its beam cutting a path through the man-made sand storm, he stumbled over chunks of concrete towards the vault door, coughing as his still-inflamed lungs rebelled against the dust. The torch beam picked out the Twisted frame and the great disc, now distorted, like some huge bent washer. With Sneiger and the four Arabs, Tippett peered into the room itself, but couldn't see too far inside for the moment.

Sneiger prodded Tippett in the back with the snout of his automatic pistol, and took the torch from his hand.

"What the fuck's this?" demanded Tippett angrily, and proceeded to cough violently.

Sneiger replied that this was as far as the 'Limies' would go.

His optimism was shattered a second later when, from inside the vault came the sound of Davis's voice and then a flood of light as the two headlamp units were plugged back onto the battery. Makmoud and the other Arabs were caught off guard, and it was to cost them dear, for their AKs were still slung over their shoulders — useless.

"An FN makes one fuckin' big hole from this range, Yank, so just stand very — very still, and behave yourselves."

Davis stepped forward, out of the gloom and into the light, the weapon in his pointing directly at the knot of surprised men. Too late Sneiger remembered Davis, he'd been with

Tippett all through, but was missing when he and the Arabs met Tippett — he'd certainly had time to drag the heavy batteries into the vault and wait there immediately after the explosion.

Sneiger's bowels contracted as he began to realise the consequences. Tippett moved behind the Arabs, sliding the Russian assault rifles from their shoulders, and removing the assorted pistols from their waistbands and holsters.

"Well, Sneiger, what did you have planned for us now?" asked the mercenary in a smooth voice, whilst gesturing to the Arabs to line up against the wall, face in, on outstretched arms. Then in a stronger voice:

"How many of them waiting for us up there, you bastard?"

The American shrugged his shoulders and stared at the floor. Davis repeated the question to the American, but got no response.

"They are expecting to hear the sound of your forty-five blowing us away, is that it? Well, don't let's disappoint them — who's first?" sneered Davis, catching the pistol that Tippett tossed to his.

The American looked up from the floor in obvious alarm as the Englishman cocked the weapon and clicked the safety catch off.

"No — " began Sneiger, "I wasn't going to kill you."

"Bollocks," replied Davis and swiftly touched the pistol to the back of the first two Arabs heads, pulling the trigger as he went. In the close confines of the passageway the noise was a physical blow to the ears.

"How many more?" asked Davis quietly.

He placed the pistol against Sneiger's temple. Sneiger's face was now streaming with sweat that streaked the dust down his cheeks.

Sneiger began softly, speaking in an almost hoarse whisper.

"How do I get out of this alive?" He ended the question with almost a plea, turning his eyes to Davis to search for clemency, to look for a chink of leniency in the man's armour.

"Tell me the answers and we'll see," replied Davis quietly,

the granite look unchanged, his mouth a savage scar on his face.

"If you know about the people on the top floor, well, that's about half of them. They've got some more anti-tank rockets, and there's a strong possibility of a road block if we don't — " He paused momentarily, and then went on, faster now as though by the spilling out of all the secrets would somehow absolve him. " — capture you all".

"What's in these boxes, and what are their numbers?"

"These are their numbers," said the American, fumbling in his top pocket for a scrap of paper. "But I don't know what they contain."

"One other thing. The shooting that killed Crofts — yours or the Moslems?"

"Christian," came the quiet reply.

Davis leaned towards the two remaining Arabs and killed them both.

"Sit down, Sneiger — over there," said Davis, his voice sounding distant and unreal to him after the second pair of gunshots had partially deafened him. Davis looked at Tippett in disgust. The American's reply had both answered a question as to his own fate and sickened Davis slightly. Sneiger sat in a corner that was adjacent to the still warm bodies of Makmoud and his three luckless companions. He kept staring at the distorted features of the Arabic leader. Davis's bullet had entered his skull at the back and had pushed one of his eyes out. The frightened American just stared at the lifeless, bloody socket, mesmerised.

Davis stood thoughtfully for a moment, then turned back to the American.

"You take this and go get your boxes, Yank, we'll settle up later. Just give me the keys to those three safes." He indicated the large grey objects that lay to the left of the safety deposit section. Sneiger looked upwards in disbelief then, pushing himself upwards quickly, he scrambled towards the grey boxes.

"I'll open them for you."

110

Tippett and Davis exchanged glances once more, then moved into the vault behind the American.

Within twenty minutes all three safes had been emptied, their contents now resting in the mound of sacklets that the mercenaries had found stacked on a table inside the safety deposit section. Sneiger had pulled the six boxes from the rack and had left them, unopened, beside the money taken from the safes. Joined by Christie, he'd then started opening the other deposit boxes, Christie sorting the paper money, which was of almost every denomination, and stuffing it into yet more of the small, canvas sacklets. The pile of documents, deeds, transferable bonds, policies, gold ornaments, icons, stamp collections and the like grew steadily beside the stack of opened, hammer-painted, blue boxes.

Sneiger began to feel safer with every passing minute. He'd not forgotten the look on Davis's face when told that Crofts had been killed by a Phalangist. Although by no means out of the woods, he had been heartened nevertheless when Christie had appeared on the scene. He'd come to see the progress and in his excitement at finding Tippett and Davis stuffing literally millions into sacks, the six boxes out on the floor and Sneiger with a fast-growing fortune in the deposit section. He'd missed the bodies of Makmoud and his companions completely. Davis told him to go back to his position but Christie ignored him completely and started working with Sneiger. Davis, rankled by the man's stupidity, made towards him, but was stopped by Tippett who caught his arm.

"Leave it, mate, there's few enough of us as it is." Davis looked at Christie for a moment, then picked up the transmitter that lay with his shirt.

He checked with Duncan, Johnson and Edwards for movement of any kind. When they replied in the negative he told them that the money was secure and that they'd start loading the truck shortly. With that he picked up several sacklets in each hand and made his way up the stairs to the Bedford.

To Sneiger, the fact that Christie either hadn't noticed the bodies or hadn't been told of the events that had occured prior

111

to his arrival in the vault was significant. Hoffman appeared to have a lot of faith in the arms dealer and had told Sneiger in London that, no matter what happened, Christie would keep to his end of the bargain and that, if the job could be successful, then Christie was the one to make it so. He'd also seen, during the time spent in the mercenaries' company that there was some animosity between Davis and Christie, and that this had manifested itself when all the spoils were there. If he could capitalise on Christies' obvious greed and cause a split in the mercenaries' camp — he might just have a chance not only of survival but also of pulling the job back together again. But he still shuddered when the picture of Davis's face floated in front of his eyes. He worked on silently and was on the point of whispering to Christie when Davis returned for more of the sacklets. Tippett had completed the emptying and stuffing and was on the point of helping Davis, when the radio crackled into life and Edwards' voice whispered:

"They're coming down."

"How many?"

"I don't know. I can hear them on the stairs."

"Johnson, if you heard that, get up there, just hold them for as long as you can. I think we've got half a chance because their leader, Makmoud, is down here, slotted, and without him they might not make too much of it."

At this news Christie turned around quickly and saw the bodies.

"When did this happen?" he said.

"Ask that little bastard," Davis replied, looking at Sneiger. Then he turned to Tippett.

"Where's that haversack, the one that has all your bits and pieces in?" Tippett indicated the spot where the bag lay. Davis moved over to it and emptied it carefully, then walked back to where the diminished pile of sacks were. He stuffed the canvas haversack full of them, and then told Sneiger to go to where the other bodies were, and sit down. When Sneiger was sitting, Davis turned to Christie and said,

"I don't know what deal you struck with Hoffman in

112

London behind our backs, and now isn't the time to sort that one out. Only one thing now, don't fuck up on me or there will be problems — for you."

Christie made as if to speak, but Davis had already turned away. He picked up the heavy 45 and went to where Sneiger sat.

"Payback time, asshole," he muttered and pushed the haversack into the man's face, jamming his head against the wall. Davis then thrust the 45 into the sack and pulled the trigger; there was no ear-shattering crash this time, just a muffled thud and the tinkling of the cartridge case as it was ejected. The American's legs pumped convulsively for a moment, and then were still.

"Let's get the stuff into the truck," said Davis, without a backward glance at the dead American. "And fucking quick. Call Johnson, Christie, and check he's in position with Edwards. Then start carting the stuff with us."

The two mercenaries began to carry the sacks up the stairs to the truck, where Duncan loaded them. From that moment they were living on borrowed time. Presumably it wouldn't take the Phalangists long to realise that something was wrong, that their leader was in trouble, that there had been no word on the radio. Davis considered using the radio, Sneiger's set, to reassure the Lebanese, but was well aware that it would probably have quite the reverse effect.

Working frantically, between the harsh glare of the head-lamps and the trucks, they waited for the inevitable descent and ensuing action. Davis never knew how long it took, he was kept too busy to calculate the suspended pause between the death of one man and the reaction of another. But at last the waiting was finished. His radio came to life again as Edwards said:

"They're coming on now."

He could see the first Arab emerging at the bottom of the east staircase, along the end of the long, wide, high-ceilinged passageway. He was satisfied that it was the only way down; the west staircase behind him, hidden by partitioned rooms, had already been too extensively damaged to be negotiable.

There were three other Arabs, who had descended in single file and then fanned out as they approached, slowly, their rifles held nonchalantly in one hand by their side in an affectation of innocence and trust. Edwards recognised the tall slim youth at the head of the approaching men and saw him raise his free hand briefly, amicably, but failed to reciprocate, dismissing the empty gesture. Behind them, from the staircase, came more Arabs. If they throw a grenade, now, at this distance, thought Edwards, they could duck into any of the rooms they were passing and miss the blast that would finish the pair of us. But it was taking the loosely packed knot of men a long time to reach the two Englishmen. Edwards' shirt felt damp on his back but, although it irritated him, he made no move. Another few seconds passed. They were gambling.

Then it was all on. No word passed between Johnson and Edwards, no sign, nothing that would betray their action but both men squeezed the triggers simultaneously. The effect was devastating and total. Two times eighteen heavy-weight bullets tore into the eight Arabs, at chest height. Not permitted time to return a single shot, the already dead man collapsed into a thrashing, screaming, convulsing tangle of blood, blood and more blood. The two mercenaries stood stock still, for a fraction of a second, shocked by the intensely painful noise that seemed to have penetrated to the very centre of their heads. With the gunfire still reverberating along the corridor, and inside their heads, both men acted with the discipline instilled into them some years before when paratroops in the British army. They both moved to a new position to await another onslaught; this time it had to be a grenade, lobbed around the corner first, so they fell back to the protection of the stairwell.

Here, both men attempted to pull their thinking together. Still unable to hear anything, Edwards, never the less sent a message to Davis that the first round was theirs "by a fucking mile". Johnson changed his magazine and quietly lit up a smoke, but said nothing to Edwards who found the man's calm

114

unnerving. Despite everything Edwards continued to find his matter-of-factness and equanimity rather intimidating. There was something remote and chilling about it, something mechanical and unapproachable. He welcomed the man's presence, but at the same time he found it discomforting. Perhaps it made him feel too obviously vulnerable and human — and he thought of his damp shirt and the moments of self-doubt before the shooting started. He couldn't imagine Johnson ever suffering the same emotions, the same and sudden failures of confidence. He looked at the mercenary again, reproachfully.

"What's happening downstairs?" he asked eventually.

"Sneiger's out of the way."

"How?"

"What does it matter?" Johnson replied irritably. His sharpness deflated the other's interest.

"What about moving down a floor?" Edwards suggested.

"You must be joking!" Johnson didn't even look back at him. "They'd be fucking swarming all over us. What's wrong anyway? Feeling nervous?"

Edwards didn't reply.

Downstairs, Christie and Davis continued to carry the bulging sacks and unopened boxes, including Hoffman's, to the waiting Bedford. They had heard the sounds of firing from the upper storey, as in all probability could the guards standing out in the square. With this in mind Duncan slipped back along the roof of the truck to the Uzi, and Tippett took up a position inside a doorway where he could cover both the yard and a good part of the roof.

From now, as they all recognised, the risks had increased immeasurably. Even if they could keep the gunmen inside the building at bay, there were always more outside, keeping the Moslem left out, but locking the mercenaries in quite as effectively. If they co-ordinated an attack the outcome would be inevitable. Makmoud already killed off." In reality, only a good slice of luck would keep them alive the rest of the day, until the welcome darkness gave them their chance to slip out of the trap. And Davis didn't relish the idea of relying on luck — in spite of the fact that his calculations (and their chances) had always depended on it. The trap, after all, was partly of their own making, and they had walked into it willingly, though not innocently. It had not been blind bravado, but nor had it been the result of a mechanical, logical assessment of favourable odds. Perfect plots, and the certainty that go with them, are fictions that fail to explain both motives and events. Davis, like the others, had been motivated primarily by an optimism that was reasonable in some respects, irrational in others. There had never been any certainty of success; but more important there had been a belief, based largely on past experience. Had it been founded on anything more theoretical, or had it relied on any simple plan of cause-and-effect and probability, then the sure consequence would be failure and extinction.

Davis was at least happy that luck had delivered the head of Makmoud but this piece of luck was overshadowed by practical events of a more decisive nature about to be played in and outside the shattered facade of the former American bank.

For almost immediately the first shots, fired from one of the buildings opposite spattered into the ground floor area in and around "Aggie". Duncan, who'd been busy distributing the sacks inside the old Bedford, climbed back onto the vehicle's roof, slid forward and, using the forward Uzi's alternatively returned fire, indiscriminately peppered the buildings across the square. Tippett, who had come to the edge of the banks ruined frontage, checked the area from the shelter of a concrete support, but after a careful scrutiny saw nothing. He shifted his gaze to the roof opposite just in time to see the back-flash from a rocket launcher, fired from an adjacent rooftop. He shouted to Duncan:

"Rocket, for fuck's sake down."

At the same time he leant back and pumped a few rounds up towards the figure on the sky-line. He never knew whether

116

or not he'd hit anybody because at that second the rocket exploded about six feet in front of the concrete pillar he was behind. The rocket exploded, sending shards of red hot steel flying in every direction, one of which caught the back of Tippett's hand, slicing it open. Duncan was not so lucky. Some of the shrapnel ricocheted off of the concrete ceiling and hit him in the back and neck. In his contortions he rolled from the roof of the truck and fell heavily, his leg twisted badly beneath him.

10

Kalter was young, in his late twenties, with short fair hair, a pleasant though not particularly handsome face, and he wore casual clothes: slacks and a pale blue pullover beneath a light grey raincoat. He carried a single leather suitcase and a plastic bag containing a magazine and three or four Russian novels.

A girl saw him off at the rainy airport and stayed behind long enough to see his plane taxi and take off, climbing impossibly into the grey skies. Then, avoiding impertinent glances, she made her way to a vast parking lot, opened the door of the stolen Citroen, and drove quickly back towards Berlin.

Kalter, wedged between a business man and a nun, took out one of the novels — *Crime and Punishment* — and sat back to suffer the tedious flight. He disliked flying immensely — which was why it would never enter his head to volunteer for a hijacking. Let the others do it! Some of them were stupid enough, or idealistic enough, to enjoy anything — whatever Ulrich, or whoever, asked them to do. It was clear that they would be happy enough to die for her and most of them, Kalter felt, eventually would, incinerated in one of their bomb factories or shot to bits in a riotous, cowboy-style gun battle with the police. That's the way they imagined the world would end, not with a whimper but a bang. It made dying glamorous and in the end what concerned them most was style. For the most part, like Kalter himself, the products of the self-conscious middle classes, ex-students, they did not want to be confused with low-class gangsters. So they were preoccupied with style, with image, with reputation, with the rhetoric of their beliefs. Kalter's own girlfriend was like that. Often, at night, she would wake him up with a desire, not for sex but for theoretical discussion. She was only sixteen and had run away from home to join the "movement" having become, in her own words, sickened by the affluence, the satisfied stupidity and complacent guilt of her family. For Kalter, when it came down to it, she was a good screw. She opened her legs for him as if he was a symbol not a man. She wanted to be impregnated by the spirit of the movement.

Kalter kept his own thoughts to himself. True, he had once, briefly, shared her radical beliefs, her consuming commitment to bring capitalism to its knees. However, it was different now. He couldn't give a fart. Capitalism — revolution — Leninism — proletariat — the triumph of the working classes — all these words and slogans were as empty as balloons. They had lost their validity; they no longer described anything in the real world.

Kalter himself was not driven to violence by such concepts but because, once he had stepped outside the bounds of conventional life, he knew he could never return. He was, even to himself, a misfit. He could not have chained himself to an occupation, to family life, to any of those values that composed an orthodox existence. He needed too much to be free — free of responsibilities, ties, obligations. The "movement" allowed him that freedom, just as it recognized his talents. For he had discovered, soon enough, that he could take life without compunction. And in the taking of life a lack of conscience was a distinct advantage. He was never betrayed by sudden disquiet or a failure of belief. He never confused human beings with symbols of oppression, hating from a distance, in abstract, by sympathizing when in contact. He had no time for the mystification of life that the others habitually indulged in. There was no mystery, merely physical experience: hard, ineluctable facts. And the simple fact remained that, no matter what a man might have thought, or done, or be expected to do, he would die if shot properly, if some internal organ was damaged irreparably, if his heart ceased to function. It was purely mechanical.

Kalter enjoyed his reputation of being a cold-blooded killer; it gave him a certain amount of prestige. The others sometimes seemed to admire what they didn't themselves possess, the selfish instinct of animal survival. He could also take professional pride in the effectiveness with which he carried out his periodic assignments. Normally, it was true, these assignments took him no further than the cities of West Germany. But occasionally he had been further afield — to Paris, twice, and once to Rome. This time his ultimate destination was London, a place new to him. He was looking forward to the visit.

In his suitcase he had a travel brochure informing him of the sights to visit, the monuments and buildings. He also had an address book with the names and addresses of a few contacts, including an old friend from his schooldays. In his breast pocket he even had a photograph of the man together with a photograph of his girlfriend in her bikini. In the lining of his raincoat, however, he had a third photograph, cut from a newspaper, of a man called Martin Hoffman.

Kalter had no idea why Hoffman, an American, had to be destroyed. He knew of the movement's rabid hatred for everything American, and it could be that this man Hoffman had close financial ties with the West German establishment. On the other hand it might have something to do with the new "alliances" everyone was talking about. It was hoped, apparently, to create close relationships between most of the world's major underground movements — an arrangement that would make each less isolated and vulnerable. Kalter himself was sceptical of the outcome: how could organizations with such different philosophies and backgrounds as the IRA, the PLO, The Baader Meinhof group and the Red Army Faction successfully work together? Nevertheless it was in the air and perhaps this particular murder was at the behest of one or another of the many guerilla organizations. Anyway, Kalter thought, who cares? Surely no-one, not even the blindest fanatic, believed that a solitary murder would alter the course of history? They just did for the sake of appearances, while history itself went its own sweet way. . .

He lit a French cigarette and threw the book back into the plastic bag. The nun beside him started to cough violently, holding her hand to her face. Oh, Jesus, he thought; but politely, carefully, he stubbed out the cigarette and closed his eyes.

11

Under cover of the new darkness and the lashing rain that boiled on the broken concrete surfaces, Tippett edged his way slowly around the square and towards the road out, feeling the ground with his undamaged hand from time to time for fear of stepping on shattered glass. At the entrance to the road he paused, and listened. Apart from occasional sounds of distant firing, he couldn't hear a sound. He edged out into the road from the square pressing his body against the wall, and waited again. Nothing. No chink of metal, no flare from a match, no footsteps. In that there was a measure of relief. On the other hand, he was more than conscious that the kind of weapons possibly now trained on the bank were not dependent on visual recognition to be effective; nor for that matter did the darkness necessarily hinder them. Depending on the sophistication of their equipment, Tippett might just have well been standing outside the building in broad daylight.

Cautiously he retraced his steps, trying to dismiss the unnerving thought. He moved as slowly as before, but this time travelling in a line he knew the truck would have to take. With infinite patience he searched for, and removed, the shards of glass and lumps of concrete in its path, the slight noise covered by the drumming, incessant, drenching rain. The sky was an inky, impenetrable black, much darker than an ordinary urban night. Tippett felt a peculiar sightlessness.

Apart from Davis in the driving seat, and Duncan stretched out in the back over the sacks of money with the machine gun, or "gimpy", poking its evil snout over the steelwork, the rest of the mercenaries waited patiently behind the truck. When Tippett returned and gave the all-clear sign the four men began to push the heavy, lumbering vehicle forwards, moving it first inch by inch, weighed down further by the accumulation of the sacks. It rolled slowly through the opening that once had sported armour-plated glass and bumped off the kerb and into the roadway that ran around the small, still fountain in the centre of the square. The rain lashed down now, lancing through the shirts of the four heaving men. Davis leaned out of the open door in an effort to see the road in the wet inky blackness, his head and shoulders hanging far out and down the truck's side in an effort to see the outline of the kerb. He could hear the grunts of the others and their gasps for breath as they struggled with the enormous weight. They could hardly be expected to go on for much longer, and even now the snail-like pace was interrupted by pauses that grew longer each time they stopped. Though they were still some way from the corner, Davis put the brake on, climbed outside and quietly told the others that they'd have to take a chance and run for it. The four men thankfully climbed over the improvised tailgate one by one, the last one to climb aboard being Christie. As he made his way into the truck's coal black interior, he stumbled over and landed heavily on Duncan's broken leg. The result couldn't have been worse. Duncan let out a shrill shriek and immediately fainted, but in doing so, clenched his hands convulsively; his injured right hand was holding the trigger mechanism of the "gimpy", and stream of bullets arced off into the night, whining into the facades of the nearby buildings in noisy ricochets.

The velvet darkness was immediately lit with flashes of fire from a dozen different places. Tracer rounds floated and disappeared into the bank, as did the larger, orange-coloured blobs of rockets. Each lit up the bank's interior for a brief second as they exploded.

The initial crash of firing had frozen Davis momentarily; then as the first rocket zeroed into the bank, he was galvanized into near panic. He frantically pulled the starter knob — but to no avail. The motor didn't even turn over. With fleeting thoughts of a bump start he suddenly realised that the ignition switch wasn't turned on. He spun the key and pulled the starter again — this time with success!

With the engine coughing, Davis roared off down the road towards the corner. He pulled the light switch out and immediately spun the steering wheel to turn the charging truck down the narrow street that turned off of the small square. His vision limited by the armour plate, and further limited by the driving rain, the only thing he could see was a wall that the truck was angling away from. As the truck squared up in the roadway proper Davis swerved and braked simultaneously. Not twenty metres in front of the sliding lorry was one of the Phalangists mini-buses angled across the roadway — a roadblock!

With his head swimming, Davis rubbed his face and tried to marshal his thoughts. Little stars kept floating and popping in front of his eyes and his forehead ached. He began to wonder where he was and what was happening. Then his mind dispelled the fog that was clouding his thoughts . . . through the inky blackness he could just make out a glimmer of light ahead.

Davis pushed himself forward and upright. Through the slit in the armour-plating he peered forwards. The light appeared to be coming from under the truck and shining forwards onto what appeared to be a bus seat. Still attempting to clear his "puggled" thoughts, the dazed mercenary wondered why the truck's engine wasn't running. He reached for the starter and turned the engine over. "Aggie" burst into life and, with the roaring engine, the final whisps of fog disappeared from Davis's brain. He jammed the gear lever into reverse and jumped the clutch out. The Bedford went backwards in a series of lurches and then stalled. With a growing sense of panic, he realised that the two vehicles were locked together by tendrils of misshapen metal. He snapped the truck into first and drove forward, then snapped the clutch in and changed into reverse again. Outside the Volkswagen was on fire, flames licking greedily from its shattered windows in tongues of vivid yellow. Davis revved the engine hard and let the clutch out quickly. The truck lurched, complained, and jumped back and free with a wrenching and splintering of tin plate and steel, its single light sending a beam upwards. Bullets, fired from an unseen position, hammered against the truck's protective side plating, sounding to the dazed and confused occupants like some giant jackhammer. Davis hit the gear lever again and drove for the gap that now presented itself between the bus and the wall. The truck didn't steer properly and hit the bus again but made it through the gap. The driver's door, with its extra protection, was ripped off and seemed to flutter away as easily as torn paper.

They were through. From the back of the truck came the sound of Duncan's machine gun, firing blindly back towards the burning coach and the unseen gunman. Davis thought he recognised the coach as one of those that had brought the Phalangists into the city, but he couldn't be sure. Certainly he had seen, illuminated by the spurting flames, other bodies beside the one on the roof, scattered across the roadway — though of course the dead gave nothing away, least of all their religion. They were just victims, and this a scene of desolation, one bright image of waste, futility and slaughter as effective as a stage set.

Davis had caught the acrid stench of burning rubber, foam and flesh, before accelerating away into the darkness. Behind him, unable to repress it, Christie had vomited over the sacks of money and himself.

A few minutes later, still heading south-east towards the hills that would take them out of the city, Aggie suddenly lurched across the road, pulling the heavy wheel out of Davis's grasp. There was a grating, abrasive sound of metal on cement as he slammed on the brake and brought the vehicle to a slithering halt at an intersection. Having apparently miraculously escaped further roadblocks and roaming gangs of Moslem gunmen — the hazards of war — they had been cursed, like an ordinary motorist in some peaceful city street, with a flat tyre.

"Shit!" Davis said loudly and bitterly. "Fucking shit!"

Gingerly feeling the lump of grazed skin on his forehead he clambered out to inspect the damage. The final shreds of rubber were just about to part company from the rim of the wheel; whatever the cost they would have to change the tyre. Climbing back into the cab he turned the limping vehicle into another street and looked for somewhere to stop that afforded a measure of cover, and was gratified to hear nothing but the grating clatter of the wheel rim. After five or six hundred yards he found what he wanted, a small plot of empty ground, bordered by a fence and containing a solitary and disused outbuilding. He drove the unwieldy, battered truck straight through the fence, which collapsed like matchwood, switched off the engine and doused the inadequate light. The others, bruised and stiff, followed him to the ground. Tippett was despatched forward, Edwards was to watch the road behind them. Davis was left to worry about lifting the monster high enough for the wheel to be changed. Lighting a welcome cigarette he went back to the cab to collect the jack which had been kept by the driver's seat in a slot cut into the floor and retained by a canvas strap. The strap was broken; the heavy-duty jack had probably been torn away with the door.

Johnson suggested constructing a narrow ramp, of timber or steel, to skid Aggie along until the front wheel was airborne. So, leaving Christie to tend to Duncan and locate the spare ammunition clips for the machine guns which had become buried in the crash, the two men started a search of the area. Around them, down the dim, drab street, most of the dwellings were virtually in ruins, as if they had been deliberately demolished in preparation for redevelopment. Some of the front walls had collapsed, revealing odd bits of tattered furniture and fireplaces, sometimes whole upper floors suspended ridiculously on thick wooden joists above the wreckage and the rubble. There were no signs or indications of life; just this endless empty wasteland, eaten away by war.

As they searched, now more accustomed to the gloom, Davis had time to reflect that they had been unusually fortunate. The trap had not shut, as it might have done, and the danger had curiously evaporated, as though it hadn't been real. By the same token, of course, wars were always full of apparent paradoxes, sublime or merely peculiar exceptions to what passed for universal laws. You only had to think about the poor, unfortunate sods in the International Brigades who died on their first day, or in their first hour, in Spain; of the soldiers who died on the last day of the war; of those who walked unthinking and safe through an enemy minefield. Moreover, Davis had seen strong men die of shock, untouched by anything but the proximity of a bullet; and he had seen men, whose bodies had been shot to pieces, survive. Wars the world over are full of such small stories, as significant in their way as any report of major offensives, great victories or defeats, if only because great victories are impersonal, whereas the fortunate or unfortunate anecdotes are individual and human and arresting. If they prove anything it is simply that blind chance, in all its perversity and perplexity, plays a greater role in human affairs than the anticipated, the planned, the carefully scheduled, the expected — the blind chance of a single, burning, inexplicable flare; of a bus consumed by flames; of a puncture . . .

Johnson, rummaging among the fallen rubble, uncovered a snapped joist which the two men dragged back across the street. They laid one end on top of a ramp made of loose, broken masonary and jammed the other under the axle. In the small outhouse they also found several unopened tins of lubricating oil, and smeared some of the fluid onto the heavy beam to help the truck's upward slide. Davis then drove the Bedford, at a perilous slant, up the gradient with comparative ease; the timber held the weight long enough for the wheel to be changed and, though it creaked and cracked as Davis reversed down, they were mobile again.

Further down the road, Edwards shivered in the cold air, waiting to be recalled. He was soaked through, and the wait had seemed eternal. He remembered odd, similar nights, one on Luneberg Heath when, as a young soldier on a NATO exercise he had stood by a ruined barn in that empty place and waited for the dawn. Then, again, in Angola, near the town of Maquela, wet and cold under the pitch black African sky, and later in Mozambique, a solitary vigil over a dead camp fire, listening for the passage of armed men through the long grass. Looking back, his life began to appear as a succession of such moments, separated in time but forming a pattern all the same. Moments of intense physical loneliness, that somehow managed to add up to something else, something more emotive, deeper, more unlooked for. He felt, suddenly, strangely, like a man who was always waiting for the light to break, and knew that his vigil, always disguised by circumstances, was some kind of spiritual loneliness. It frightened him slightly. He had not thought to come to such conclusions, and it didn't fit with the extrovert he was always taken to be. But it was true enough, this hollowness inside, and the recognition was also gratifying. It allowed him to understand so much, to make a pattern of his fractured life.

He lit another cigarette and shivered. Somewhere behind him the truck's engine broke into throaty life.

12

Kalter was supposed to book into a small hotel on the Rue de Hautville. The "movement" (it was only called a "gang", deliberately, in the European press) disliked personal indulgences of any kind, though with its cultivated, Bohemian image it always habituated the popular haunts of the young, the trendy, the superficially artistic. Kalter was therefore well aware of what kind of hotel the Hautville would turn out to be, and he had no intention of staying there even for one night. As it was he planned to stay in Paris at least for two nights, before catching the boat train to Dover, for he had an old connection in the splendid city.

So, ignoring his orders, he booked instead into one of the large, expensive hotels in the Rue de Monmartre. There, he relaxed in his elegant room with a large brandy and tried to decide which of the many pleasures on offer in the Parisian streets appeared most tempting. It was, of course, already very late but that was of no consequence, especially here. The only thing you couldn't get in Paris, late at night, was a good meal; most of the restaurants, reflecting traditional domestic routine, shut early. But never mind. There were always the clubs, the cafes, the street life, the brothels. Kalter had already experienced them all, for he was a man of epicurean tastes who did not stint his sensual pleasures. He was extravagant, arrogant and he lacked what in others he found puzzling — sometimes annoying — a deep, ineluctable sense of guilt. Moreover there was something innocent about him too, sitting easily beside the corruption that would have made him an excellent officer in Hitler's SS. It was the innocence, however, of the solipsist, the spoiled child who has little sense of the reality or purpose or separateness of others. In many respects Kalter had never grown up, had never reached the age of responsibility. His selfishness, his lack of self-doubt, his brutish and single-minded passage through life — all these things made him good at what he did, but for very little else. There was not a touch of kindness, of compassion, in his make-up, not a shred of simple, unaffected decency. Like a child picking the legs off a spider he remained indifferent to any feelings that were not his own.

He thought fondly, now, of all the places he might visit, and even contemplated contacting the "connection" — the woman with whom, during his last assignment, he had had a brief and violent affair. He assumed that she would still be there for him even if, in the meantime, she had been silly enough to marry. Women, he recognised, were like that: at bottom they were sentimental and clinging. They were terrified of freedom. They needed to load themselves with obligations and burdens, to suffer. Somehow they never knew they were alive until they forced themselves to suffer.

She had been very beautiful, although her face looked as if it might belong to the type which eventually goes out of fashion. Her legs were long. She had always worn boots — and a bright raincoat.

She was probably married now — to some quiet and respectable urbanite who furnished her with a house and car and a child in exchange for a milder sexuality.

He wouldn't call her after all. She would only disillusion and disappoint him. He would go out and look elsewhere, possibly get drunk. It didn't matter. In the end nothing, beyond brute survival, mattered very much or at all. Everything existed, but nothing had any value.

He pured a second, generous brandy and knocked it back. Then slipping the raincoat over his shoulders he strolled confidently out into the Parisian night, watching the warm clusters of neonlights glimmer invitingly before him. Soon, as if he had walked into a hall of mirrors, the night swallowed him up.

130

13

Conscious that another flat tyre would be fatal to their chances of escape, and equally aware of the roar of the engine in the subdued streets of Beirut, Davis slowed down to a walking pace, the engine barely ticking over. Aggie lurched clumsily over the flotsam and jetsam of war, carrying its silent and pensive passengers, the single headlamp sending its crazy, angled beam away into the distance. Davis was frequently forced to leave the sanctuary of the wall to avoid larger obstructions, and eventually, reaching an intersection, he found the road ahead completely blocked by the bullet-riddled carcass of a Mercedes car.

He stopped the Bedford and consulted one of the maps provided by Sneiger, with the aid of a torch. Theoretically, he decided, the left-hand fork should lead them through to the coastal road again, and the Christian sections of the city.

After a whispered conference with Tippett, who was still nursing his injured hand, Davis coaxed the vehicle around the corner and continued travelling along a street that seemed, in the partial beam, to have suffered less than those around it. Shortly, indeed, he knew that they had entered a more fashionable and expensive inner-suburb, for the houses were set back further from the road, and some were protected by great iron gates. The road itself was relatively clear of debris and masonry as though, Davis thought, even gunmen perversely respect the privacy of the rich and only bomb their own; as if all wars, whatever the ostensible cause, were also always class wars.

The lack of material damage, the sense of returning to undisturbed normality, probably caused a lapse of concentration, made Davis feel easier, safer, more nearly out of danger. Suddenly, the front wheel rode up an unseen obstruction and, as the truck slammed down hard, the solitary headlamp flickered and died. Davis, unsighted, was forced to stop. He switched off the engine.

"What's wrong now?" Tippett muttered. "Everything's going fucking wrong!"

Davis, extracting the torch, but shading it to a thin pencil beam, turned round in his seat and let it play, briefly, over the faces and figures behind.

"Headlamp's gone," he said wearily. "Nothing else we can do until morning. It should be light . . ." He studied the luminous dial on his watch. ". . . in about three hours. We ought to get some kip."

"We'd better get a couple of guys out as minders," Tippett said.

The torch light had picked out the pasty faces of Duncan, who was semi-conscious now from pain and morphine, and Christie. Edwards also looked exhausted and almost unwell, and Davis himself was well aware of the need for sleep after the tortuous drive.

"Thanks for volunteering," he told Tippett. "You and Johnson take the first hour. Then wake me up."

The two mercenaries took up positions, one in front, one behind, about fifty metres from the truck. It had stopped raining, but there was still no moon, nothing but the wet velvet night wrapping them around. Tippett, the forward guard, decided to venture a little further. Slowly, his left hand never breaking contact with the high wall, the FN held in the other, he felt his way down the narrow, gloomy street. After about three hundred yards he ran out of wall and, groping blindly, nearly lost his balance as he stepped off the wide kerb. Crouching down, he ran his hand over the smooth corner of the stone, realising that he had reached some kind of junction. At first he thought that the minor road he had walked up now joined a major road going from east to west. But after crossing it he found another corner, and the remains of some sort of shop front. He was in a square, having entered it from one corner.

Keeping one foot in the gutter and the other on the kerb he moved, crab-like, along its western side. Suddenly he froze. Away to his left, but not far away, he heard the rasping sound of a match being struck repeatedly, then catching, flaring and guttering at once. Tippett, stock-still, savoured the rush of blood through his heart, the surge of adrenalin. Then, half-crouching, he moved again.

Some fifty yards further his right foot found another turn of the kerb, this time moving away to his right. Cautiously he crossed over again to the centre of the square, sure now that the road encompassed it entirely. He stopped and, peering around a low iron fence, looked once more in the direction he'd seen the flaring match. Briefly he caught sight of the glowing end of the cigarette twenty yards away and, satisfied, he returned stealthily and by touch to the wrecked shop-front. Once there he pulled the walkie-talkie from his belt, turned the volume control down to its lowest point, and switched on the slim radio. Slowly he twisted the volume switch up until the faint noise of static was just audible, and whispering urgently he called the truck.

For Davis, as for Tippett, the meaning of the incident was immediately and disturbing clear. There was a manned road-block at the edge of the square — but no way of determining its size or sophistication.

Telling Tippett to remain where he was for the moment, Davis called in Johnson and the two men discussed the situation in tense undertones. Neither wanted to attempt any movement until first light, and Davis made it plain that he had no intention of turning back in an attempt to find another route out of the city. He produced the map.

"At least," he said, shining the torch over the labyrinth of streets, "we don't have to go through the roadblock. We go here — " He indicated the route with his finger. " — directly across it from below, leaving us vulnerable only for ten seconds or thereabouts.

"Johnson, you, Edwards and Tippett, take three of the rockets. I'll pick up at the corner of the square afterwards, then whatever happens we're getting out of there fucking quick."

"Okay," Johnson said simply. "We'll get off now. In about an hour we'll give you a buzz. Five seconds later we'll start firing."

Waking the sleeping Edwards, Johnson slipped from the open cab, collecting the three rockets from beneath the seat. Within seconds the two mercenaries had been swallowed up by the darkness, and Davis could only wait.

The sky began to lighten and, by Davis's watch, it was around four-thirty in the morning. Davis was surprised when Johnson failed to make contact, but decided against using the radio himself. Instead he woke Christie, who was nestling at the rear of the truck with his FN protruding out of the narrow gun port. Duncan stirred and moaned softly, secretly, but failed to open his eyes. You poor sod, Davis thought.

At ten minutes to five his radio crackled to life. He turned the ignition and Aggie moved forward, gathering speed. Ahead, in the deep purple early morning sky he saw, in rapid succession, two vivid backflashes as the rockets were discharged, the noise of their impact lost inside the rattling truck. The third rocket went off just as Davis turned, at speed, into the opening of the square, and this time he heard the rewarding explosion and spotted, through the thin slit that passed for a windscreen, the thick mushroom of smoke rising above the barricade. At the same time, the three mercenaries broke from their positions on the central island and raced towards the truck. Davis slowed down to allow them to climb over the tail-gate, anxiously looking towards the barricade, noticing the two cars angled across the road, one of them brightly burning.

"Get fucking moving!" Tippett was shouting. Davis thumped his foot down on the accelerator.

"It's an armoured car," Johnson said calmly, taking Christie's place at the back of the truck and poking his machine gun through the slit. "We missed it."

"It was my fault," Edwards said suddenly. "I should have . . ."

"Just shut up," snapped Johnson. "We'll get it."

The road out of the square was wide and empty and straight. It sloped downwards slightly, increasing Aggie's speed. Davis knew he had to make a right turn, but he couldn't see any turnings. He felt his throat constrict, his mouth dry with apprehension.

"Come on!" he told the truck. "Come on!"

Edwards began firing seconds later, spraying the road behind them. Davis could imagine the armoured car emerging into vision, its turret swivelling, lowering as the gunner found his aim. At the same moment he saw the turning, probably only fifty yards ahead. He braked hard and swung the truck across so they were broadside when six thirty-calibre rounds passed through the protective steel plating as though it were made of polythene.

The first round passed an inch above Tippett's head, a fragment of it slicing its way down the side of his neck and burying itself in his shoulder. The rest of it, distorted out of all recognisable shape, tore through Edwards' torso and shattered his spine, killing him instantly. The next two rounds passed cleanly through the back of the truck, touching nothing inside, but the final three rounds turned Aggie into a charnel house. The fourth hit Christie in the chest, creating an enormous cavity, and the fifth passed through his stomach and bowels, loosening them as he crashed backwards lifelessly, the bullet ricocheting off the steel plates and drilling through Tippett's heel. The final round went low through the steel, was somehow deflected upwards and opened Davis's thigh from hip bone to knee. Still not spent, it continued into the engine compartment, narrowly missing the distributor but lodging itself in the side of the radiator.

Davis didn't feel the pain. He didn't even notice, till later, that he'd been hit. But at the back of the truck, in the semi-darkness, as the heavy rounds whined and ricocheted, warm gushings of blood soaked the dry sacks of money and bills, someone screamed with unaccustomed pain, and Edwards' open and surprised eyes gazed upwards, blankly, towards the roof and beyond it.

Johnson, miraculously untouched, continued to fire, shouting. "Fuckers, fuckers, fuckers!" until he was hoarse and the clip was empty and the blood had spattered across his chest and arms. He shouted back to Davis:

"Turn the first corner you come to. I'll nail the bastard!"

Davis might have preferred to keep going, but he knew that Johnson was right. They couldn't afford not to stop the armoured car, even if, with only one rocket remaining, their chances were bleak. A moment later he scraped the truck around a narrow opening and stopped, arresting the motor. Johnson was already on the ground, the LAWS rocket primed. He lay down facing the street, half-tucked behind the wall, his FN beside him and the rocket at his shoulder.

Those that were still alive heard the loud crash that seemed first to indicate a hit, but then the sharp, staccato bangs of the rifle which seemed equally to refute it. Johnson reappeared. With no sign of emotion he told Tippett and Davis that they were alright: it had been a hit, and he was just making sure.

Davis, conscious now of the gaping wound in his leg, drove away. Soon, lost in the labyrinth of unfamiliar streets, he felt himself growing faint as the blood, forced out by the pressure of his foot on the accelerator, pumped out thickly over his thighs and drenched his trousers.

"Someone give me a jab," he said. "I'm fucking shot."

Tippett, crawling over, stuck the needle into his arm.

"You look bad," he said solicitously.

"I think the bone's OK. How about you?"

Tippet grunted.

"I'm OK."

Davis grimaced, tightening his grip on the wheel, and

watched the road shimmer unsteadily, blearily, in the distance.

"I could have got round that fucking corner," he said quietly.

There was a pause. Then he felt Tippett's hand on his shoulder, gripping it hard.

"It wasn't your fault, mate. Just one of those things. We'll survive."

"Edwards?"

Tippett looked back, but knew already.

"No. Not him. Christie's dead too. There's blood everywhere, and shit."

Davis thought of Edwards, remembering things, glad of the unexpected company of Tippett's companionship. He thought of Christie.

"This . . . this is stupid," he said, "but, just look in Christie's pockets, will you? Will you?"

Tippett slithered back down the truck, while Davis waited impatiently.

"Anything?"

"Yes. Diamonds. Hundreds. In a handkerchief."

"I knew it." Despite everything, Davis found himself laughing, without really knowing why. "Makes me feel better," he said.

Daylight, brightening the streets, had brought the fat flies with it, droning over the bodies. There were a few people about, watching curiously disappearing. A child ran out in front of the truck and Davis, in a dream, swerved and missed it.

"Know your way around, then?" Tippett wondered lightly.

"What do you think?" Davis laughed again, slowing down. "Sure I do."

"I never thought otherwise," Tippett said.

They were approaching another intersection — perhaps, inevitably another roadblock.

"This is where we turn right, isn't it?"

"Of course it is," Tippett said. "I told you."

The truck swung round the steep bend, finding no obstruction, and straightened out. And ahead of them, beyond the last houses, the road began to climb gently, taking them away from Beirut.

14

Hoffman couldn't get through to Chamoun. There were no messages. Sneiger had disappeared off the face of the earth. Beirut might as well have been a small island somewhere in the Pacific. But, yes, they assured him, they were trying to re-connect the cut lines. There had been trouble — more fighting and so on. But then again these things happened even at the best of times.

The American waited a whole day before making his call to Washington. There, he met not only with exasperation, but also with incomprehension, and he was finally and brusquely directed to report to his contact in the Embassy the next morning.

On the news that evening, and in the papers the following morning, there were reports (as there often were, of course) of fresh fighting between rival militia in the Lebanese capital of Beirut. One report even mentioned that some of the heaviest fighting had taken place in the famous, but now largely deserted, banking quarter, only recently occupied by the Moslem left. According to this particular source, a group of Phalangists had briefly attempted to reoccupy the sector but, for some reason, had withdrawn after sporadic fighting. A spokesman for the PLO confirmed that the area was still in their hands, and suggested that the attack had been a diver-sionary tactic, designed to deflect attention from the ruthless shelling of Palestinian refugee camps. The report finally had realistically pointed out that, because of the volatile, confused state of affairs persisting in Beirut, there was little hope of determining the truth on this or any other occasion. Both sides continued to issue contradictory statements and, in any case, since the fighting was frequently between small, private armies, it was difficult for anyone, even the leaders of the major factions, to determine exactly the cause or outcome of individual encounters. The truth, as always, remained hidden behind political rhetoric, disguised by the very nature of urban guerilla warfare.

There was little comfort in any of this for Hoffman, who began to believe that Sneiger had mishandled the operation. Either that or Chamoun, for his own reasons, had betrayed a trust, withdrawn his troops early and left the mercenaries to the mercy of the Palestinians.

The next morning, in the dismal London rain, he took a taxi to Grosvenor Square and reflected how his entire career, which had been built upon the sands of political and economic convenience, now hung in the balance. Despite everything — despite the many successful financial operations, the clandestine deals — he had no protection against failure. A single mistake weighed more heavily, reduced what they would call his viability, his use to them. At the same time, ironically, he would prove most useful in defeat since, as a scapegoat, he would save them embarrassment. They gave him responsibilities only in so far as it left them free of the consequences. Blame was always handed down, deferred, settling heavily on those who depended on favours.

Inside the building, an elderly, white-haired, mild-mannered American called Roberts invited him to take a seat and relax.

"We don't want you getting the wrong idea," said Roberts, with a smile that looked genuine. He combed the thick white mane back with his hand, and put his feet up on the brown leather top of the mahogany desk. Hoffman remained silent.

"I gather," Roberts went on smoothly, "that you've heard nothing."

"Not as yet."

"I see." Roberts lifted his hands and placed his fingers

together in a steeple, bringing the spire close to his chin. He looked closely at Hoffman, an unbroken gesture that revealed small, shrewd eyes an unaffected habit of observation. The steeple collapsed abruptly.

"It seems," he said, "that Chamoun withdrew his men early."

"That's what the newspapers said."

"Well, if the newspapers can get information . . ." Roberts left the mild accusation unfinished. "You had a man there."

"Yes. Sneiger."

"Any good?"

Hoffman paused, as if the true answer interested him.

"In the past, yes," he replied.

"Look — " another bleak smile " — we're not questioning your judgement. It's just —"

Hoffman interrupted, "— that when something goes wrong some people start to look around."

Roberts leaned forward.

"Has something gone wrong?"

"It could have. Stupid to deny it. I should have heard by now."

"Indeed. Cigarette?"

"Thanks. No."

"I've flipped through your files — you know, just refreshing my memory," the white-haired man examined his socks, just visible between cuff and shoe. "Many, many good things. Israel needs friends. There are . . . many enemies."

"Yes," Hoffman said.

"Those boxes . . . important. You know, papers . . ." Roberts shook his head.

"I didn't know," Hoffman said evenly.

"Just papers, records . . . if they . . . if Arafat . . . an important place, Beirut, to us, to them. If the Christians lose — imagine."

"Are you telling me that we're financing Chamoun?"

"I'm not telling you anything. Just the papers."

"I ought to know — something."

141

"Always better to know nothing." At last, leaning awkwardly forward, Roberts opened a small wooden box with his fingers, found a cigarette, lit it. "After such knowledge, what forgiveness?"

"I don't know." Hoffman's eyes skirted the spartan room with its single, framed photograph, of a woman standing by a lake. Canada perhaps. Vermont. "Your wife?"

"Yes. Dead now. Cancer. A long time ago . . . You're not?"

"No."

"Maybe you're right. Get used to it. The loneliness is awful, if you have. You know, just that one person all that time. The next thing, gone, switched off like a light."

"I'm sorry."

Roberts' laugh made a brittle sound.

"No. It's not so important. Not real anymore, you understand. Not real."

Pale light seeped in through the high window, splashed on the wall. It was still raining.

"And the papers?" insisted Hoffman, pressing.

"Papers. Just papers. Don't ask about the papers."

"Why worry about Arafat? Look, it wouldn't surprise him. America — Israel — Chamoun — a natural chain."

"Other things. Things that shouldn't be written down. American politicians — always in writing, you know, everything listed, filed, noted, minuted, the lot."

"I know. Government by committee. Isn't that why democracies are always unsafe? Too open?"

Roberts killed the half-smoked cigarette in a clean glass ashtray.

"Hate smoking," he said. "Vile. I wanted to tell you, Chamoun pulled his men out."

"You know? You've heard?"

"Of course. There are always others. You and . . ."

"Thank you."

"Don't pretend to be shy of the truth. On the outside you can't afford to be. Still, it's their business to keep you guessing, isn't it? . . . Chamoun heard rumours, just rumours, that the

Syrians were going in. They had tanks. It was in the air. He wouldn't wait."

"But the papers?"

"Oh, he never knew about the papers. Just the money, the property . . . his friends, you know."

"So what happened."

Roberts shrugged, slapped his thigh unexpectedly, looked up.

"Chamoun had men in the bank. On the roof. Kids, gunmen, who knows? The killing started. There was a fire-escape."

"Not on the plans, the photographs," protested Hoffman.

"I suppose not. A government regulation. Put in later. Just before the Palestinians went in. Ironic."

"Very."

"Anyway, they skiddaddled. That was it. Chamoun says he thinks the Syrians or the Murabitoun or God-knows-who went straight back in. Arafat's crowing."

"Anything else?"

"Nothing. That's how it is. Armies of the night."

"Too many plots."

"Oh, always plots, you know that. Games. Really. Isn't it?"

"And the papers?"

"The end-game, you might say. Forget about them."

Hoffman, uncomfortable, thought things through.

"And chance . . .?"

"That it might have worked? Sneiger, those English guys? Sure, why not?"

"You don't know?"

"No more, in effect, than the newspapers. What do all the satellites and telexes and computers in the world mean when you put them besides barbarity?"

"But it's unlikely. It must be. Without support . . . the plan was to . . ."

"No," Roberts put up his hand. "No. Don't tell me. There are some things I don't want to know. Everyone does what they can think of. It doesn't matter now, does it?"

143

"And if they get back?"

"That's up to you. They've nothing against you. The papers mean nothing to them. They'll give them up. Oh, of course, Chamoun's looking all over the place. He's made promises."

"And if, let's say, Arafat has the papers?"

"One thing I'll tell you. Chamoun's finished. There's too much. Nothing else."

"If there's nothing else, I'll go." Hoffman started to get up.

"Sit down, Martin!" A strange, intrusive, somehow familiar note in his voice Hoffman thought, almost suspicious. He noticed the flickering smile again.

"What are your plans?"

"Not *my* plans, Mr Roberts . . ."

"No games, please," Roberts stiffened visibly.

"I'm here, or was to be, for another two weeks. Then New York. Then . . ."

"Then we'll tell you. We have something in mind. A West German bank wants . . . advice, the kind you give. Hm?"

"You'll let me know?"

"Naturally. In due time. I want you to read a number of reports first. Collect them from my secretary as you go out. Interesting. One of those things."

Hoffman felt some of the tension drain from his body, felt himself relax with the relief of being wanted, after all. But he was also resentful that he needed it — bitter from the good fortune of a slave.

"Anything else?" he asked.

"Don't think so, Hoffman. Only — you fucked up. I know it, you know it, other people know it."

"I thought . . ."

"Don't bother. How much are they worth? You fucked up. Your arrangements — the whole thing. An incompetent shambles. Everyone's got mud on their faces, shit even. You know?"

"If I *had* known . . . the papers. Why me? It wasn't my job."

"Precisely why. Not your job. But Sneiger's . . ."

"Sneiger?"

"Sneiger," Roberts repeated. "Sneiger knew. From somewhere else. I was told."

"Armies of the night," Hoffman said, fatuously.

"You wouldn't know."

Hoffman nodded.

"That's right. I wouldn't. I wouldn't know anything about the Deuxième Bureau, the spies, the agents, provocateurs, terrorists, gangsters, gunmen. No, I wouldn't. I know about money, physical things — the times of ships, the weight of guns, the market and the special price for cartridges, missiles, tanks, planes."

"Perhaps after all, it was someone else's fault. A miscalculation. Mine perhaps. Or someone in some other office. Here in Cairo, Tel Aviv, Washington, who knows?"

Roberts offered his hand.

"Well, goodbye. If something else comes up . . ." he shrugged. "My wife also said to expect the unexpected. She was a healthy woman. You know?"

Hoffman walked back out into the rain, and decided not to get a taxi. He strolled slowly towards Berkeley Square, under the dripping trees, watching remotely the other passers-by, under their black umbrellas, hurrying towards an appointment, a lover, a friend. He had always valued his own loneliness, and never felt it. He had always walked on the other side of the road, unhindered by familiar contacts. There was no possibility of catching a glimpse of a friend, by accident, in a crowded city thoroughfare, for he had no friends, just acquaintances. He had never been married, and it had not occurred to him to ask why. It hadn't mattered.

He walked on. Soon his suit, underneath his light coat, was discoloured with damp. He stopped, thinking where to go to. There was nowhere. Nowhere, at least, he wanted to go. Just ahead of him a young couple also stopped. They were laughing at some private, unheard, trivial joke. The boy put his arms around the girl's shoulders, drawing her up close, pressing his lips to hers, cutting off the laughter. As he moved on past them, looking away, Hoffman's heart was bitter. He had lost something, some capacity or instinct or emotion that was routine but elusive. He stopped again, to find out where he was. The sign at the end of the road merely indicated that he was a mile from Piccadilly Circus.

15

They had stopped somewhere to the side of the road, in a shallow ravine beside a small olive grove. In front of them, sparkling in sunlight, lay the sea, a light green expanse of passive, untroubled water.

Christie and Edwards had been roughly buried, side by side, beneath a pile of stones over which fat blue flies swarmed and feasted. Tippett had wanted to burn the bodies, but there was little chance of anyone finding them for days, weeks perhaps. In any case, without uniforms, with empty pockets, they were simply anonymous corpses, innocent or guilty victims of a spreading war.

Davis had been carried, unconscious, from the cab and laid on the ground, his feverish body covered with a blanket. Johnson, the only uninjured member of the party, washed his wounds — as he did those of Tippett and Duncan — with sea water, ignoring the moans of pain as the salt stung. Tippett still had sharpnel embedded in his arm. With the aid of morphine and a small penknife, Johnson began to dig for the lead splinters, exposing them with deep incisions then fishing them out with his fingers. There was nothing that could be done, however, for Duncan, except to bind a piece of wood to his broken leg in a crude splint. The two bullets had passed clean through his shoulder, shattering the collar bone. Johnson was afraid that, without proper medical attention, gangrene would soon set in; the wounds are already badly inflamed and weeping, the skin around them discoloured and puffy. He bandaged the shoulder as best he could and administered the last of the morphine. When the pain returned there would be no way of relieving it.

Now, they needed food as much as medical care. And beyond food they required another means of transport. To carry on in Aggie would be suicidal. Looking around at the mostly unconscious figures around him, shaded by the trucks metal side, he wondered if it was worth thinking about anyway. What was the point? In the space of sixty seconds, or less, after having run through hell virtually untouched, all the hopes and high expectations, the dreams of affluence, had been crippled in the blind chatter of gunfire. The money was soiled by blood, by excrement, by the warm slippery gush of internal organs. And how was it to be spent, under a pile of stones?

The sun went down, huge and red, into the sea. The air cooled. The landscape around him, rich and fertile, grew mellow with the evening's colours, changing its tint. The twilight sky, a deep, rich blue, glittered with an unfamiliar plenitude of stars. Watching these things, feeling the chill of the night air, Johnson knew he was alive. Beyond anything, beyond the torpid or feverish murmurrings of mutilated men, he knew that. And since he, and they, were still alive then everything was still necessary: food, another vehicle to carry them onwards, everything was important. It would be immeasurably stupid to think of what lay behind, or in front — what roadblocks or new wounds or deaths, even his own. Those were the things that didn't matter. Sufficient now to move, to hunt, to survive, to go on, to bury those that were dead and tend those that weren't.

Tippett was the first to awake. He groaned, sat up, touched the bandaged shoulder gingerly.

"Still alive," he said cheerfully.

Johnson laughed.

Tippett glanced uneasily towards the ground at the front of the truck.

"How's Davis?"

"Still alive,"

"What a bastard, wasn't it? A fucking armoured car. A fucking great armoured car."

Smiling grimly to himself in the gathering darkness, Johnson said softly:

"The way it goes."

"Yeah, sure. Bad luck. A bit of bad luck with a barrel attached to it."

"The way it goes," Johnson repeated.

"At least," Tippett managed, "we're rich now. All of us."

"At least . . . are you hungry?"

"Fucking starving. What have you got?"

Johnson discovered a touch of humour.

"Steak. Salad. Cheesecake. A glass of wine. I'll call the waiter."

Amused, Tippett said:

"He's at another table."

Johnson inspected the ground.

"If only you could eat money!"

Letting it pass, Tippet threw the blanket off his legs and stood up unsteadily.

"Shouldn't we be legging it?"

"Leave now?" Johnson shook his head. "We're as safe here as anywhere. And those blokes need to sleep. In the morning I'll try to find some food and get another van or something. It's fucking crazy to go on in that thing."

"Alright. My watch. Get some kip."

"Just what I was thinking."

Johnson lay down and wrapped himself in the thin blanket, gazing for a moment at the inky, spangled sky. Blackness folded him in, obliterating stars, and he fell into a deep, restful, tranquil sleep.

When he woke it was to find the same sky touched with bitter pink, the cold, delicate glow of the early dawn. Tippett, too, had dozed off, understandingly, and Johnson left him sleeping, carefully slipping out of the blanket and collecting his rifle before stealing away, following the track back up towards the road.

149

Turning left, away from Beirut, he began to walk. He walked for two long miles, seeing nothing but sea and sky and the narrow ribbon of the causeway snaking away. Not a single car passed by. But he could hardly turn back. Eventually, and satisfyingly, he found what he'd been looking for. By the roadside, in front of two roan-coloured VW vans, a group of traders (probably refugees, he thought) were setting up three low tables, wooden planks laid across sandbags and drums. He would have preferred to investigate them more thoroughly by crossing the road and circling round, but there was insufficient cover; he would have had to retrace his steps by almost half a mile before being able to cross safely and without being seen. So, instead, hidden from view, he watched them carry out a miscellany of household goods — wicker chairs, lamps, cushions, fabrics, rugs, icons, books and boxes of smaller items — and carefully arrange them on top of two of the surfaces. The two Arabic women in the party, veiled but loquacious, fussed endlessly over the uninteresting domestic junk, moving objects to and fro, standing back from time to time to inspect the arrangement, as if they were arranging delicate flowers in a vase. They sent back bits and pieces — a broken stool, a small portrait — calling for others, equally shabby, to replace them.

The five men, ranging in age from, Johnson estimated, sixteen to seventy, worked uncomplainingly, fetching and carrying at the dictates of sudden whims. Not far away two small children, a girl and a boy, played impatiently in the dirt, scuffing it with their bare feet.

On the third table the women laid out a pitifully small supply of cheeses, fruits, bread, and wine in goat-skins, unwrapping each article, except the wine, from coloured cloths. The food attracted the children who circled hungrily, though at a careful distance, around the table. One of the older men eventually chased them off with shouts and a raised stick, before himself taking a sliver of white cheese and munching on it with obvious relish.

Johnson continued to observe them for a while as they settled down to wait for customers. It seemed unlikely that they would find any here, for the road was still deserted and their offerings were poor and uninviting. Yet it was clear that this was their life, or what was left of it. The war, as it drove people away from their homes and cities, and as it brought about the complete collapse of the economy, making both money and labour redundant, had left them gypsies and scavengers sustained only by that infinite capacity for hope which was always most visible when there was no reason for it.

Now, as they waited patiently, sometimes scanning the empty road, they made no effort to amuse themselves but sat, for the most part, silently, passively in the shade. One of the younger men, however, fetched something from the back of the rear van and unwrapping it carefully, laid it across his knees and began to polish the black, banana-shaped magazine. The gun was a Russian-made AK, and Johnson reflected that where there was one there were probably others. Even poor traders had cause for constant vigilance, for protection against the other nomadic families who roamed, in their trucks and cars, across the spoiled, ravaged land.

He put his own rifle carefully under a bush and began to walk towards them slowly. Almost at once the children saw him and ran back to the tables where the women gathered them up. The man with the AK stood with his back to the van, holding the gun casually, with both hands, down against his thigh. The older man placed himself officiously behind the tables with the furniture, rubbing his hands together like a shopkeeper opening for business.

His Arabic greetings were lost on the tall mercenary who indicated, as well as he could with his hands, that he was interested in purchasing food and wine. The old man's eyes narrowed suspiciously and he continued to chatter volubly, as if doubting the stranger's incomprehension. He gripped a measure of richly-coloured material between brown, gnarled fingers, holding it up for inspection. Johnson shook his head, remembering to smile. He pointed again to the cheeses. The Arab, turning away, spat into the dust, but shuffled over to the last table where flies fed greedily, hazily on the bruised, ripe fruits, the vile-smelling cheeses.

The mercenary made his selection, putting the word "dollars" in the form of a question.

The Arab held up ten fingers, closed his fists, and repeated the gesture. Johnson held up ten, compromised on fifteen and extracted the money from his back pocket. In the other pocket, unseen he had a roll of fifty one-hundred-dollar bills, taken from one of the sacks on the floor of the truck.

He pointed to one of the stationary vans and repeated the question. The Arab, puzzled, looked over his shoulder, saw the women there and grinned, salaciously displaying a mouth of broken, blackened teeth. He measured out their worth, with slow deliberation, on his fingers. Then added,

"Dollars," in English.

Johnson shook his head.

"No, the van . . . the bus," and gripped, and turned, an invisible steering wheel.

Two of the other younger men, approaching cautiously, began to chatter to the elder. After a while he appeared to understand — but it was one of the others who said "no", and made a crude, dismissive gesture, ushering the Englishman away.

Johnson produced the tight wad of notes, displayed them, counted them, one by one. Once again the Arabs conferred, their gestures theatrical, their voices raised as if in argument. Johnson noted that their companion, the one with the AK, remained where he was, watching impassively.

The argument resolved, the old man held out his hand. Nothing more was said. Johnson hesitated. In the first place he felt he ought to haggle, since that would seem to them a natural response and defer suspicion. And yet, having seen all the money, they were unlikely to accept just part of it. He was a stranger. He was alone and unarmed — and they were poor and hungry and probably desperate. Even if they'd been honest once, they were almost certainly callous and indifferent now. On the other hand, of course, once he'd given them the money there was nothing to prevent them taking the same course of action and retaining the van. It didn't matter that they would have the money to buy a hundred more. At least, it might not matter, because in certain circumstances you cannot set a rational decision beside an instinct born of necessity.

After a moment, with a shrug that disguised his apprehension, he handed the money over and watched the old man count it, his eyes glittering beneath the swelling cataracts. It was so much! Surely, staggered by their good fortune, they would allow him to take the battered old van without protest?

Picking up the cloths containing the cheese and fruit, the cheap vinegary wine, Johnson began to move round the tables towards it. He was conscious of curious eyes; even the children had stopped to stare at the peculiar unforeseen drama. The van was empty, its windows smeared with dirt, its tyres worn as smooth as glass. Johnson opened the door. He heard the breaking murmur of voices behind him, then a more abrupt, obdurate sound, the release of a safety catch. The Arab motioned him away from the door with the rifle and came closer, letting it jut forward. He said something quietly in Arabic and then:

"Not yours. Understand? You go fuck away."

"I bought it," Johnson said. "It's mine."

"No. You leave. Okay? Understand?"

"Bastard."

The man grinned maliciously.

"Not buy," he said, with a brief shrug, "what's money? To us . . . no. Nothing. Leave. I shoot," he waved the barrel pointedly. "Understand?"

"Sure. I understand. Thanks."

Johnson turned, started to walk back over the open ground towards the clump of bushes, expecting to die. A truck went past, along the road towards Beirut, but didn't stop. The green, spiked leaves of the bush seemed to recede away into the blue distance. In his anger he knew he should not have come alone, that his optimism had been reckless, banal, romantic.

He reached them. Suddenly, strangely, he was out of sight, behind the thick tangle of scrub, and there was the sea in front of him and no levelled gun behind. He walked on, then turned

153

and went back and found the FN and moved the safety catch forward to the 'F' slot. You silly bastards, he thought, with grim satisfaction. You ought to have known better!

He crawled slowly along the ground to his left, found an opening and moved forward, pleased to find the positions of the group unchanged, the young man with the AK still lounging against the rear van. He brought the gun to his shoulder and sighted it, taking a long time to be sure, reminding himself that he had time for one shot, two at most. The Arab lit a cigarette, lent the rifle against his hip. One of the children screamed with delight. The old man raised his stick and the women, huddled together, whispered to one another. These last things . . .

One bullet was enough, entering the heart as if it had been the centre of a target, flooding it with blood. The Arab, with the cigarette still glued between his lips, fell forward soundlessly, his hand absurdly covering the wound. The others, momentarily paralysed — not by fear but by surprise — gazed at the dying man, didn't at first see Johnson break cover and race forward, until the women started to squeal harshly.

The four remaining Arabs, arranged together, made no movement towards the fallen gun. And only the old man spoke, shouting at the women in Arabic to be still, then spitting reflectively. The mercenary ushered them away from the vans.

"I told them we should kill you," the old man said in English. "They wouldn't listen. You see what happens when you don't listen to the voice of wisdom?" He spat again, then rubbed his mouth. "The keys are inside. Take the truck. No need for more killing. One is enough. One is always enough."

Looking back as he drove away, Johnson saw the old man appear in the road, holding the body in his arms.

16

Two days after arriving in Paris, Kalter caught the night ferry across the English Channel. The water was calm and though the night was cold, he spent much of the voyage standing by the leeside railings, watching the sea slushing against the painted metal and thinking how little he had enjoyed his visit to the French capital after all. He had met a young English-woman there who had been friendly and pleasant; they had walked through the parks, visited the Rodin museum, and then he had treated her to an expensive meal, with champagne, at a fashionable restaurant on the left Bank. After that they had wandered along the pavement by the side of the Seine, talking of nothing, and kissed, finally, beneath an equestrian statue in the darkness. Her warm laughter had encouraged him. Slip-ping a hand beneath her jacket he had felt her small, free breasts, had kissed them quickly through the protection of wool. Everything had been satisfactorily predictable, obeying a common pattern, the patient logic that produced, after all the right gestures had been made, the little moans of pleasure, the fatuously open mouth.

They had taken a taxi back to her hotel.

"How long are you staying?" she wanted to know, licking his neck, giggling.

"A few days. Who knows?"

"Business trip?"

"Yes."

"And your wife?"

"I'm not married."

155

"Oh, yes. I know."

The irony had slightly annoyed him.

"It's true. I'm not."

She had looked at him, her big brown eyes sparkling with mischief, and made a little, sly smile.

"But *I* am! That's why I'm here — to get away, before I'm too old or too pregnant to have fun. You know what I mean? It's important to escape. I'll never be satisfied being a dreary old housewife. I told him as well. He knows I'm still crazy. I want to get drunk and do all those things you can only do when you're still young. You know what I mean?"

"So you came to Paris."

"I love Paris. I was here before, with a boy. Of course it was just sex. Nothing else. I didn't know him and he wasn't interested in me. That's why it was nice. Just for a change, you know? Just letting go, having fun, not bothering."

"Ah, yes," he had said, "we are very similar."

"You're very strong," she whispered. "Ever so."

"Thank you."

"I like strong men. They make me feel — like a woman. You know?"

He didn't reply, noticing that the driver was watching them in the mirror. He leaned over and kissed her, pushing her head back against the leather seat.

"Can I see you again?"

"Sure," he said, "why not?"

Laughing again she had wiped a smear of lipstick from his mouth. The taxi stopped.

"This is my hotel."

"Yes. Closer than mine."

"I suppose yours is very — chère. N'est-ce pas?"

"A little."

"Kiss me again," she had murmured, the pink top of her tongue protruding, then slipping into his mouth. Her hand, apparently accidentally, had brushed the front of his trousers.

"God," she had said, breaking away. "You're good. Very."

And like a fool he had smiled complacently.

156

She opened the door of the taxi.

"Wait!" he had said. "Just —"

"Bye, darling."

The door was suddenly shut in his face. She had given a little, mocking wave before the taxi pulled away, and he had watched her disappear through the swing doors into the foyer of her own, expensive hotel.

Remembering it now, as the clumsy boat ploughed steadily on towards Dover, he found that time had not erased the bitterness and the shame. Some cheap English tart had upstaged him, and he could still feel the sting of the crass humiliation. Bourgeois women! Bitches! Shitholes. Cunts.

He went back inside, to the bar. The Scottish barman in a dirty white jacket, looked virtually asleep. His hair was greasy and unwashed, his cheeks covered in rough stubble. There was dirt behind his over-long, almost effeminate finger nails. Even his manner, brutish though it was, was also quite affected.

"Whisky." Kalter said stiffly.

The man roused himself with difficulty, cleaned a glass and poured a careful measure.

"Ice?"

"Nein."

"What?"

"Nein. And I said double."

"Did you now . . . heh? Scotch on the scotch."

"Look," Kalter said, "this is your job — such as it is. Maybe you want to keep it."

"That's right, sir, it's my job."

"In Germany, people do their jobs properly, decently."

"Or else, eh?"

"Or else they don't have one."

"Nice place."

Kalter restrained himself and drank the whisky. The barman, wiping a long glass, watched him.

"I'm sorry," he said after a while.

Kalter looked up and put his own empty glass back on the table.

"Fuck off." (in German).

17

For a whole day, in the courtyard of the American bank in Beirut, the stench of burning flesh persisted. No-one could remember ordering the cremation, and as usual no-one was prepared to accept any responsibility for the vile scene. Nevertheless, as a result of some whimsical inspiration, the nine bodies, their clothes soaked in petrol, continued to burn, and a few of the Palestinian guards continued to observe it, out of boredom or curiousity, ignoring the smell.

When questioned, none of them could remember much about the dead men. all found inside the bank. Undoubtedly, they agreed, some of them were armed elements of the Christian right, but others were probably Moslems, killed in the original assault. Their shrugs indicated that it was a matter of indifference: a man's religion is a trivial thing once he is dead. In fact all they could remember was itself a trivial fact: as they brought the bodies out and laid them on the pyre they noticed that one of the men was smiling. But that was that. Just a curiousity. Someone had remarked on it. Then they had started the fire.

Turning north, Johnson drove towards the town of Jubail. It had taken some time to transfer the sacks of money and unopened boxes from one vehicle to another, and even then they had had to abandon many of them, leaving them in the carefully concealed Bedford. So it was now early afternoon.

The injured men had revived considerably, though Duncan

was still in great pain, and lapsed occasionally into unconsciousness. Davis, by comparison, was relatively cheerful and some of the colour had even returned to his cheeks. The fever had passed and his leg, beneath the thick bandages, caused him no more than constant discomfort. Like Tippett he was glad to be alive, and he even allowed himself a vague sense of optimism as the van careered along the narrow, grey strip of tarmac, unhindered, towards another country.

During the afternoon they passed through three small towns — Jubail, Jelail and Batroun — stopping only for petrol along the way. Just outside Batroun, however, they ran across another road-block, manned by a single Arab in a camouflage smock and Keffi-yah headdress who sauntered arrogantly in front of the van, holding his rifle over his head. Resisting the impulse to make a run for it, Davis had slowed down and simply waved and shouted to the Arab to move out of the road. The bluff had worked. After a hesitant moment the young man had shrugged, stepped back and let him through.

The three mercenaries had discussed the best way back, but were in disagreement. Tippett wanted to drive on to Tripoli. Davis, fearing border controls, had already marked on the map a number of small, likely-looking fishing ports along the coast where he assumed they could charter a boat to take them back across to Cyprus. Finally Tippett had acquiesced.

"Nothing to lose by asking," he grumbled sourly.

Then Tippett suggested breaking open Hoffman's precious boxes.

"I'd like to find out whether it was worth it."

"No," Davis said, "not now."

"Don't you care?"

Davis paused, pulling on his cigarette.

"Would you believe me if I said I couldn't give a fuck?"

"No."

"Well, maybe I don't."

"Why not, then?"

"Just . . . I don't know. Forget it."

"As you like."

Davis spread the map across his knees and studied it.

"In another ten kilometres or so there's a place we can stop. It's probably nothing — a village — but there may be boats. There should be a junction. The road to the right goes inland to Besharre. That's where we turn off."

Johnson nodded.

"What are you going to do with the money?" Tippett asked, unexpectedly. "I've been thinking."

"I'm sure you have," Davis said. "That's all you think about."

"No. I mean really."

"I'll probably go away somewhere."

"Where?"

"It doesn't matter."

Tippett treated the idea as a joke.

"I don't believe you, mate."

"That's because you've no imagination. Anyway, mate, we're not home yet. Hadn't you noticed?"

The other man grunted.

"I said you were always right!"

"Then you ought to listen to yourself more often — Look! Down there! The turning."

The track wound down, for perhaps a mile, to the sea. There, clustered together, a few small, white-washed houses composed a tiny village set on the very lip of the shore. Beneath them two or three wooden jetties protruded out over the water, and tied to one, rocking gently against it, was a tall, white and apparently new glass-fibre cabin-cruiser.

The young soldier at the road-block was having second thoughts about the German van. It wasn't that he was in any way suspicious — only that he'd failed to perform his simple function and let them through. At first it hadn't bothered him. On a busy day nobody checks every car, nor is it expected that they will. It was really a question of presence — a reminder that, through certain areas, people could not travel at will or with impunity. There was a new power in the land.

But there had been little traffic that day. Unusually quiet, really, hardly even any refugees for some reason, with their pathetic belongings stuffed everywhere, the children bawling, the men frightened. So he had time to remember each vehicle, and somehow the one he remembered most clearly was the van with the two men in front, the one waving him out of the road. That was why he remembered. He had stepped back as if it had been Chamoun himself, or some dignitary or other. Just impulse, he decided. Let them through, no trouble, no arguments. Had they looked as if they would cause trouble? He couldn't remember. It had happened just like that. He could hardly even remember their faces.

Yet he continued to think about them. Then he remembered a message about an armoured truck. He had been told to report if he saw a truck that looked like a tank. He had been told to report if he saw a group of men in a truck. Well, he had not seen any armoured trucks, but there might have been other men in the back of the van. How did he know? Maybe the same men in a different thing. Who could tell? He couldn't report every truck and every group of men. They wouldn't want him to. Still, perhaps today he should have checked.

Eventually, though with some misgivings, he told them on the radio about the van and the two men. He told them the van had driven through without stopping. He couldn't shoot everyone who did that! Some people always ignored the blocks. They were more frightened of stopping. But he told them he hadn't seen a truck that looked like a tank. It was very quiet today, he said. Not even any refugees . . .

18

The young woman who answered the door wore faded jeans, plimsolls, a thin blue shirt and a yellow scarf tied around her neck. Her long, dark hair fell over her shoulders in a thick and luxurious cascade, and her small face, with its wide hazel eyes and pouting lips, was at once pretty and rather mousy. She spoke fluent English, though with a strong French accent, and her first response on seeing the surprise registered on Johnson's face was to laugh, brightly and appealingly.

"Oh, I expected someone else," she said quickly, though she appeared anything but disconcerted.

"So did I," Johnson replied.

She laughed again.

"English?"

"Yes."

"That's where I went to school. In London. Anyway, how can I help you?"

"Well," began the mercenary, "it's a bit difficult. I saw your boat and —"

"Not *my* boat," she interrupted.

"Your house was the nearest, so I. . . ."

"Oh, nothing here is mine. It belongs to my husband."

"Is he here?"

She shook her head. There was something quick and nervous about all her gestures — something childish, innocent. Somehow she seemed completely out of place here, as if she had been left behind after a holiday.

"No." she said, "he's away, as always. Why don't you come

in for a moment? Please. . . . Have something to drink, no?"

Johnson hesitated. He couldn't very well introduce her to the rest of the party, now waiting in the van at the back of the house, but they would expect him to report back almost at once.

The woman seemed to detect his uncertainty.

"Ah, I'm sorry . . . you are in a hurry."

"No. Thank you. I think I could do with a drink."

"Bon. Come along. For me too, a drink would be nice."

He followed her through the small, tidy kitchen into the living room with its bay window that looked out over the sea. Despite the simple, white-washed interior the room was big and comfortable and charming. There were curtained wooden cabinets, chintzy covered chairs, bronze lamps, thick white Persian rugs on the floor and a number of modern, abstract paintings around the walls. The furniture seemed to reflect not only a certain affluence but also a cosmopolitan life, as if it had been collected and transported here from countless different places. The room could have been anywhere. He sat down in a deep cushioned chair and watched her open out one of the cabinets and extract two cut glass tumblers. The shelves were stocked with bottles.

"Brandy?"

"Yes. Thanks."

She poured out liberal measures and put the tumblers down on a small glass table between them.

"Salut."

"Cheers."

The glasses chinked on contact. She smiled. But as he sipped the fine brandy he was conscious of her curious attention, of being inspected and placed. He wondered how best to explain.

"You said something . . . about the boat?" Her precocity made her direct.

He nodded, put down the glass.

"I was hoping to buy it."

"To buy it?" Again she burst into laughter. "Why?"

"Because we need it."

"Oh." Something about his expression made her frown. She looked at him with greater seriousness.

"Who are 'we'?" she asked after a few seconds, during which time she took a longer sip of brandy.

"Just friends," he said.

"I see. Here? Outside? These friends . . ."

"Yes. In the car."

She stood up abruptly and walked over to the window. There were flowers in a vase on the white sill, the faint sounds of the sea beyond. Not glancing around, she murmured:

"And how much would you pay for the boat?"

"Half a million dollars."

There was a protracted pause, a stillness.

"Why so much? You know it's too much. My husband wanted to sell it. There was an offer, not so much . . . he nearly accepted."

"I told you. We need it."

She turned round slowly to face him across the room, tucking her hands into her pockets.

"I ought to ask you something."

He shook his head, standing up too.

"It doesn't concern you."

"Are you in trouble?"

"It doesn't concern you. We need the boat."

"There are patrols, sometimes. Gunboats."

"We know."

She walked towards him.

"Will you take it anyway?"

He didn't reply but she accepted the answer with a slight nod, and could see what it might mean.

"Give me fifty thousand dollars for the boat. I won't accept more. The price includes full tanks, a few charts. Do you understand?"

"Yes."

"Bring your friends into the house. You should leave after dark, in about two hours. That's safer."

"I ought to tell you something," he said frankly, "about

the men in the car. They —"

She interrupted him with a sharp, dismissive gesture.

"Just fetch them. Go on."

The mercenary held out his hand and took hers, as if to say what she wouldn't allow him to articulate, that he was grateful, and relieved not to have to go through the pantomime of tying her up, gagging her, cutting the telephone wires, and all the rest of it.

Her own hand was small and slim and delicate like porcelain in his, though its grip was firm and certain. Once more, in the privacy of the moment, she smiled at him. Perhaps he was wrong, but behind the smile he thought he saw another message, a failed hope, a frail anticipation that had been shattered just as quickly as it had grown in her lonely imagination. He knew he should have asked her why she was unhappy. Instead he had thought only of securing the boat, by whatever means, had not considered what this unexpected, unlikely encounter might have meant for her. But her smile was brave enough, as though she accepted the foolishness of her possible fantasy, and even found an irony in the cold reality of the truth.

He left her and went back outside.

"What the fuck's happening?" demanded Davis. "We can't stay here."

"I've bought it. We're leaving in a couple of hours, after nightfall. Come in and have a brandy."

"A brandy?"

"Sure. Don't you want one?"

"I can smell it on your breath," Davis retorted, opening the door and climbing out stiffly, with a grimace of pain. He turned and began to pull the FN out, having found it made an admirable walking stick.

"Better leave that," Johnson said. "No guns."

"Don't be stupid!" Davis said sharply. "I'm not going anywhere without it now."

Johnson folded his arms and waited.

"No guns," he repeated quietly but with emphasis. "I trust

165

her. Do you understand that?"

Davis held the other man's gaze for a few seconds, then shrugged.

"If you say so."

Tippett helped Davis to hobble round the house to the kitchen door where they waited for Johnson, who carried the unconscious Duncan. Turning sideways to get the slumped figure through the narrow entrance, Johnson led the way through to the dining room where the young Frenchwoman, her hair now tied behind in a loose pony-tail, was waiting for them.

19

Hoffman's decision was, in the end, not so hard to make. He had anticipated a long, troubled night of the most painful soul-searching, a night of putting in the balance the things he was certain to lose and those he might gain, once he was free. As it turned out he found that he had already made the decision, that he had unconsciously, perhaps during that long walk through the London rain, made up his mind. Now resignation, in all its apparent bitter-sweetness, seemed nothing more than a mere formality, a question of putting pen to paper.

On reflection he realised that, as he had walked down the steps of the white Embassy building in Grosvenor Square, he had also been walking out of his own life. He had not known it at the time, for at first, of course, he had simply felt angry and afraid, and helpless in the face of the increasingly impersonal power he served so obseqiously. Then the anger and bitterness had faded pathetically, and he had only felt afraid and lonely. It had come to him, as he meandered slowly along the busy thoroughfares and over the wet grass in the deserted parks, that he was invisible, a man without a private or interior life. He was nothing but an empty husk, a shell, and his ambitions had been measured in chronicles of wasted time.

He had not known where to go. That was the first clue. He had felt listless, purposeless, haunted by the sense that he was due somewhere without remembering or knowing where. He had looked into a thousand empty rooms. His loneliness was not that of the unrecognised figure, the solitary, but that of the public man, the functionary, who disappears in private, who only exists at meetings, on the telephone, in a public bar, a hotel foyer, an airport lounge. By himself, in the emptiness of a London park, he failed to cast a shadow.

That night he composed a simple letter of resignation, addressing it personally to Roberts. He said nothing in the letter that would have explained his decision; Roberts would undoubtedly assume that it was the result of criticism and a failure of nerve. It didn't matter. What they thought was their own business. Tomorrow he would take it by hand to the Embassy. Of course, there would be the usual enquiries, questions, demands. He would probably have to report back to Washington. Still, whatever they said, it was over, he was free. And then, perhaps, he could start again, not from the beginning but from somewhere, trying to recognise the face in the mirror for what it was, trying to understand his loneliness. Naturally he would never change altogether; he was perfectly well aware that nearly everyone is a victim of their fatal consistency. Nevertheless, with his circumstances changed, his ambitions gone, he might transform his life a little. It would be far from easy, but there was always, always, that second chance.

He was a disappointed man. All his life he would be a disappointed man and now, to add to that, he would be lonelier than ever. But at least he would know his own failings, disappointments, his loneliness, would feel these things on his pulse. Could he live with that? He didn't know. He would try.

He thumbed through the collection of records in the flat, finally selecting Mahler's first symphony and laying back on the bed to listen. Throughout the entire piece the telephone failed to ring, where once its insistence had been perpetual. For a while at least they had quietly dropped him from the circuit, a loose wire in a box of gadgets.

After the record was finished he fell into a dreamless sleep.

Kalter, disembarking from the train at Victoria station, queued impatiently for a London taxi then order it to drive to

Blake's hotel in Chelsea. It was raining. He had been told that it always rained in England.

He checked in at the desk, went upstairs to unpack, then put through a call to his contact whose address was somewhere in Pimlico. They spoke in German, but the only information relayed was the time for Kalter's social call. It was also tactfully implied, however, that Hoffman was still at the flat in Knightsbridge, that the plan could proceed smoothly.

With a curt "danke", Kalter replaced the receiver, fetched his coat from behind the door and ripped open the red lining, taking out the photograph. It was so typical, he thought, that they had not supplied a better, clearer one. This looked at least three years old, and there was no way of telling. Hoffman might have grown a beard, lost his hair, or grown fatter around the jowls. But no, he thought, don't worry about that. There were too many other ways of making sure. Be patient . . . and this time will be like the last.

He contacted reception and asked if there was a public swimming bath in the area. Apparently there was, so he asked for a taxi, changed his clothes, collected a towel and took the lift down to the lobby. After the baths he planned to go on to a gymnasium if possible, for a good work-out, then on into Soho. Someone had given him a free pass to a number of clubs. Some of them, apparently, were no more than gambling dens, others just expensive cocktail bars. But he had been reliably informed that one or two offered more adventurous and exotic fare — far more realistic, in fact, than the more visible haunts advertised by neon signs and curling photographs.

He promised himself, in short, a good evening out, hopefully culminating in someone else's bed. Already the memory of the evening in Paris was fading, obliterated by his optimism. As a hunter he was incorrigible, and a woman was a victim just as much as the men he assassinated. Moreover, the sensations were not dissimilar, for he had known before now the sexual thrill of murder, the eroticism of killing. Why also should orgasm be called "a little death"?

The taxi was waiting. Handing in his key, gripping the rolled white towel, he walked out into the innocent day.

20

Outside the windows, where the sea gently roughed against the freshly painted wooden jetty, it was growing darker. The girl, collecting the glasses, put them into the sink and then came back into the room and nodded to Davis.

"You should leave now," she said softly. "This is a good time."

Johnson was already standing by the van, scanning the open fields behind the house intently as he had been doing for the past two hours when he hadn't been familiarising himself with the controls of impressively powerful launch. Up till now, however, he had made no effort to transfer the sacks and boxes and guns. He had seen an occasional figure stepping out in front of one of the other houses and wander down to the shore. Clearly none of them were aware of anything unusual happening in the house a hundred yards from theirs, but no doubt the situation would have changed had they seen the mercenaries ferrying objects out to the boat. It had been better to wait — even though the waiting had begun to make them all slightly anxious again.

Nevertheless the young Frenchwoman had over-ridden their protests and done her best to tend to the wounded, even tearing up one of her sheets for bandages and handing around a spare supply of antibiotics she'd found in a bathroom cupboard. Duncan had returned to consciousness under the careful ministrations, but had relapsed after a few minutes of muted agony. The girl had insisted that he stay behind. She said she knew of a doctor who would treat him and keep his own mouth shut afterwards. Then she would simply buy a passage for him on one of the local fishing-boats.

"What about your husband?" Davis wondered. For the first time her expression turned cold.

"That's none of your business," she snapped back. "I've told you what I can arrange."

Davis studied the unconscious man, dressed now in a fresh and laundered shirt, who was shivering on the chintz-covered sofa.

"Thanks for the offer," he replied thoughtfully, "and you might be right. I don't know. But we're taking him with us."

She had accepted the decision without protest, but now, at the point of their departure, she began to fret again. Wasn't it better, she argued, to leave a live friend behind than carry a dead one? She was sure she could keep his presence a secret for just one or two days, even if people were looking for them. Not that she wanted to know what they'd done.

"But, I quote you something," she said. " 'There are some things, some things that are not worth looking into too deeply.' Do you understand?"

Davis smiled, sealing the understanding. Then, without another word to the woman, he hobbled with Tippett's help to the door.

"I'll stand guard," he told Johnson. "I'm not much use for anything else. Just get that fucking stuff in quick."

The two men began to carry the sacks from the van to the unlit boat. After a few journeys they had grown more sure of the path and could walk without stumbling, though Tippett's damaged arm continued to slow down their progress. Davis, the FN cradled in his arms, studied the exposed area up to the main road. At least he would see any approaching headlights — and did on two occasions, the cars or trucks moving swiftly past towards the distant city.

An hour passed. The night, moonless and cold, closed in around them. Davis could hear the men's footsteps across the wooden planks of the jetty, the creak as the boat listed gently,

171

the sea as it slapped against it. A few lights went on in the neighbouring houses, but no face appeared at the windows and no doors opened.

"How much longer?" he asked Tippett as the mercenary plodded by an another repetitive trip.

"Not long. A few sacks — the boxes — not much left."

"Just the boxes. Leave the rest of the sacks."

"But —"

"Just leave them."

"Alright."

"And tell Johnson to carry Duncan out to the boat."

Tippett paused fractionally.

"I agree with her," he said evenly. "There's no point."

"Yeah. I'm sure. But why not me as well? I can't fucking walk either."

"You know what I mean."

"Yeah. I know."

The other man still hesitated.

"Well?"

"Well nothing. He goes with us. That's it."

"You're wrong, Davis."

"I don't give a shit. You know what it is. It might be you, or me — it might have been Edwards."

"Then it would be just the same."

"Just bad luck."

"One of those things."

Davis glared venomously into the man's face.

"You know, there are some things you can do something about. You know? It's not just good or bad luck. It's never just one of those things. You'll find that out someday."

Tippett turned away sharply, continued down the path to the boat, stopped suddenly as he heard the crack of a single shot behind him. Davis heard it too and stiffened, bringing the FN round. He pressed himself against the wall and peered helplessly into the darkness, swearing softly under his breath. Just a single shot, then nothing, the return of the silence, but different now, pregnant with danger. The shot had hit nothing but it must have come from somewhere near the road — it must have.

Johnson joined him by the wall.

"What is it?"

"I don't know. I don't fucking know."

"My gun's still in the van. I'll have to get it."

Crouching down, the mercenary started towards the van a mere twenty yards away, around the corner of the house. Then the Frenchwoman appeared and stood for a second in the light at the kitchen door.

"Get away!" Davis hissed urgently. "The light!"

She closed the door hurriedly behind her.

"I heard something," she whispered, and Davis, close to, could see the apprehension and alarm in her soft eyes.

"Someone fired a gun — up there. Do they often . . .?"

"Never before. I'm frightened."

"Get back inside."

"Perhaps I could talk to them. . . . Oh, I don't know what to do."

Davis smiled.

"Neither do I."

Tippett and Johnson, approaching from different directions, joined them, Johnson holding two FNs.

"What now?"

"Go now," the girl implored them.

"I want one of those boxes. And I want Duncan," Davis said harshly.

"If someone covers me I'll go for the box first," Johnson replied. "You should get down to the boat, Davis."

"No. I'll try and cover you from here. If I have to run then I'll run. Tippett, you'll have to try and carry Duncan down there. Think you can make it?"

"If you can run . . ."

The two men slipped away. There were three further seconds of silence. Then a second shot shattered a window pane, passing through into the room beyond.

The Frenchwoman gasped, broke away, ran forward, and

shouted out in Arabic. Davis could see her standing at the edge of the field, apparently listening. She shouted again. There was no reply. He wanted to call her back but couldn't. He watched her move forward, further into the darkness, until it swallowed her up. Suddenly he saw her again, running towards the house, slipping, falling, shrieking as she fell but running again . . .

"Jesus Christ," he thought, watching it all in slow motion, all the time it took for her to cover that short stretch of grass, her chalk-white face, and then the sudden, harsh clatter of the guns. Bullets laced across the field, spattered against the sides of the house, breaking glass in showers, thuding into the house. She fell again, impossibly, riddled, shot to pieces by the fusillade, her body jerking convulsively, slithering a few more feet. But by that time Davis and Tippett were firing back, raking the gentle slope, seeing nothing, firing blindly. "Jesus Christ," thought Davis, seeing her punctured body. "Not again."

The gunmen, whoever, whatever they were, had apparently spread themselves in a shallow arc across the field in front of the house, some taking shelter behind a low and crumbling wall Davis had noted earlier. It seemed that they had not, so far at least, ventured further down to either side of the exposed house. Perhaps there were only five or six of them — not enough for an effective pincer movement.

Davis, sensing the gash in his leg opening again, the warm blood running down into his boot, moved painfully forward and crouched behind a pile of rubble obviously intended for the foundations of a nascent extension. He checked his remaining ammunition and heard the quick clatter of Johnson's FN, the whine of bullets hitting stonework. The kitchen door opened and shut almost noiselessly; glancing round he saw Tippett struggling to hoist the inert form of Duncan over his shoulder, then move away down towards the waiting boat. The FN jarred against his shoulder as he pulled the trigger, pumping out a stream of bullets. A shadowy figure, passing across his field of vision, seemed to fall and disappear, only to be replaced by others, suddenly visible as they ran forward, firing, blistering the facade of the building, melting away again into the thick gloom.

Davis looked back. There was no sign of Tippett. He wiped the sweat out of his eyes and looked again, canvassing the ground to either side of the narrow path. He saw the tall mercenary rising off the ground, as if in silhouette, saw him take hold of something, a pair of arms, and move backwards dragging his companion. The most cursory of glances told him that Tippett had been hurt, probably badly. He wondered why, if that was so, Tippett continued to labour with the unconscious body. Then he understood, and almost smiled to himself.

They were firing again, steadily, along the arc. He listened to the bullets strafe the van, breaking its windows, clattering against steel. For a while, a few seconds, Johnson returned the murderous fire, then the FN went silent. At that exact moment, a bullet hit the wall in front of him, glanced off and nicked the side of Davis' head above the right ear, wetting his cheek with blood. Other bullets flew off the masonry, pinning him down.

From the blackness below he heard the twin engines of the boat break into throaty life, the water bubbling under the stern. He hesitated. He might have heard Tippett calling out, but couldn't be sure. The pain in his leg was unbearable and the blood had drenched his trousers, which now clung to his skin. He started to crawl forward, skirting the small barricade, towards the corner of the house. As he turned the corner he was hit again, the bullet passing through the bone of the shin, splintering it. Then he was behind the van, temporarily sheltered. His hands touched something, solid, warm, unfamiliar, and at his touch the body of Tippett rolled gently over, almost into his outstretched arms.

"You stupid cunt," he whispered, tousling the dead man's curly hair. "It's all over for you."

He stood up, trembling with the effort, pulled himself to the rear of the van and sought with his fingers for one of the metal boxes. He lifted it and turned and started to walk back along the path, dragging his leg. His vision kept blurring, as sweat poured down his face. He was in plain view now, but the shooting had stopped and he stumbled on in the blindness of his pain and the inevitability of his death, feeling the ground slope away beneath him. For five yards, ten, fifteen. The boat's engines, the turbulent water, sounded as loud as his own heartbeats. He could make out the shape of the boat. He could see the water frothing, turning over white and black. And then he stopped to see the boat move, coaxed away from the jetty, its sides chaffing against the wood. The roar from its engines increased, subsided, built again as it edged out darkly. No, he thought, No. But he stood and watched and didn't shout, felt the world start to turn slowly under his lame feet.

The boat buffeted the end of the jetty, slipped out into the dark channel, began to turn, straightened and moved away. As he sank to his knees he lost the sound, then caught it once more again in the distance, the blood beat in his ears, then darkness.

Guenta and Monika Meyer lived in rented accommodation — four rooms on the second floor of a large, shabby whitewashed terrace house between Victoria Station and Besborough Gardens. The area was unfashionable, lower middle class and despite its centrality it had the dispirited, characterless air of a remote, unlovely suburb. Some of the houses were even boarded up and empty; others already demolished.

The interior of the Meyers' residence proved to be as dilapidated and seedy as its crumbling facade, and Kalter found himself introduced into a gloomy, high-ceilinged hallway cluttered with an ancient and battered pram, innumerable broken toys and an old bicycle with a buckled front wheel. The Regency wallpaper, faded and peeling in places, had probably been put up in the thirties and the stairwell smelled damply of improperly washed nappies, boiled cabbage and neglect.

Kalter's nose wrinkled with disgust. Unlike his friends in the 'movement', he was no longer able or prepared to glamorise or pity the anonymous masses of the under-privileged. Kalter was not surprised to find the Meyers sheltering behind this unimpressively authentic facade. It was perfectly in line with their assumed identity as urbanities, their desire for an ordinariness that everyone else spent their lives trying to escape from. Moreover, the fact that they had ended up in some run-down (but once elegant and smart) Georgian town house was equally revealing. They were not the kind to commit themselves totally to the culture they so forcefully espoused and defended (at least in the past), to move out to a sprawling estate in a grey, dismal suburb. This faced elegance was their compromise, and what set them apart was that they continued to confuse a working-class culture with their Bohemian, vaguely raffish past in Kreuzberg, one of the oldest, poorest areas in Berlin. Kalter had first met them then, when as early members of a group called the Hash Rebels they had lived in the Wieland Commune and fallen under the spell of the supposedly charismatic Rudi Deutschke. In those days, of course, back in the futile sixties, love had been more important than war, mescaline more important than molotovs. But things had changed quickly. Sporadic, inconsequential, anarchistic acts of violence turned into a campaign of terror; the Hash Rebels became The June 2nd Movement and the bombings, murders, bank raids and recriminations started. Soon afterwards, having lost his right hand because of a badly made molotov cocktail, Guenter had left Berlin for London, taking his girlfriend with him. They were still "legal"; the German police had nothing concrete against them, and in any case Guenter had proved an incompetent urban guerilla. He was all for the counter-revolution so long as it meant no more than drugs and music and a change in sexual habits. Yet even that turned sour, with Monika's accidental pregnancy and miscarriage. Finally, however, it was the clumsy, farcical episode with the bomb that had convinced him of his inability to survive the expediences of the new society.

All this had underscored for Kalter the dilettante nature of the whole "underground" movement, for which he had nothing but contempt and which, he was sure, would prevent it ever coming to anything in a political way. It was all style, an experiment, a fantasy, a game. And Guenter was not the only one to have grown tired, or frightened, or just bewildered; to have run away as though, after all, it was possible to abandon and ignore the cherished class struggle. Others, of course, were already dead or in jail, the persistent victims of their own myths. It wouldn't be long before the rest either grew bored of being hunted, or got themselves shot up in a final melodramatic effort to preserve and sanctify those myths that were beginning to look fraudulent and empty. Part of the myth, after all, had depended on the vulnerability of the State itself, the ease with which it could be rocked to its foundations by small, disciplined groups of saboteurs. But the State, after its initial disbelief, had proved resilient and contemptuous — more callous and more mercenary, more brutal and much more effective than the Hash Rebels and the student mobs. And, secretly, Kalter was gratified that this was so. He could admire and respect a militant and a strong State, just as an ordinary criminal can respect the laws he feels obliged to break. He was clever: he had no ideals and there was nothing he cared enough about to die for. He was no martyr.

Monika let him in. She was wearing a loose bath robe and had wrapped a large towel around her wet hair. He could hear bath water escaping and the faint sounds of music from a radio. She smiled at him with an effort at sincerity, but it was immediately obvious from her manner how little she relished the role of providing a safe house for visitors from the past. It was not an obligation either of them could escape from easily, but there was clearly little pleasure in meeting it. Kalter found himself regarded as if he was a ghost, a haunting reminder of how the past continues to inhabit and disgrace the present.

"Come in, Klaus. Guenter is getting dressed. Sit down. A drink?"

She was addressing him, unexpectedly, in English.

"No, thank you."

He sat down in a large and battered leather armchair, the

178

arms shredded by a cat's insistent claws, and tried not to contemplate the rest of the dismal, second-hand decor. The woman, tall and thin and nervous, moved around uncertainly between the pieces of furniture, deprived of her function as hostess.

Guenter came in. He wore corduroy trousers and a collarless shirt and his fleshed-out features sported a new and thickening beard. His hair was cropped short. He offered his left hand, awkwardly, and even made a move to embrace his old comrade, self-consciously drawing back at the last moment.

"Why haven't you offered Klaus a drink?" he demanded, covering his own embarrassment.

"I don't want one."

"For me, a beer." Guenter sat down and put the false, gloved hand on his knee. Another ghost, Kalter thought irreverently.

"Good to see you again," Guenter said. "Many times we think of you — and Rudi — and Kreuzberg."

Kalter smiled thinly but didn't reply. Monika came back with an opened can of beer, and Guenter began again:

"Just the other day, when . . ." He stopped abruptly, uncomfortably. "We heard about Georg, and Ulrike. Just the newspapers. We wanted to ask you. . . ."

"Ulrike was raped in her cell, before she was murdered," Kalter replied flatly. "Everyone knows. They don't pretend too much."

Guenter exchanged glances with his wife.

Kalter shrugged. "What do you expect? It's the same law for everyone."

"No," Guenter shook his head. "How can it be so, Klaus? They're the murderers. Sometimes, I know, they give us guns and explosives just for an excuse. They arrange things — even the drugs."

"What do you expect?" Kalter repeated patiently. "Politeness? Decency? Honour?"

Guenter's eyes registered his sudden confusion.

"But they're like the fascists," he said. "We prove it. All this

179

pretence of freedom and change . . . underneath they're the same men."

"How simple you make it sound. Like good and evil. In the old days, perhaps . . ." Kalter paused, conscious of implying a criticism. Guenter continued.

"Now, everything is confused, changed. So much killing. That's why we left. After Georg came back from Jordan, then it happened. I remember Monika and I were at a party in Kreuzberg. The pigs came in, with machine-guns. One of them said: 'Are you Guenter Meyer?' He had a photograph so I said yes. He said: 'We won't arrest you now. Where is Baumann?' They have photographs of all of us already. And Baumann told me there was a provocateur in our group, some-one close to us. That's what the pigs were doing. You could trust no-one."

"I never do," Kalter remarked complacently. "It's much better that way."

"So much, then, for the new society," Monika Meyer said bitterly, observing them both. "No trust. No decency." She turned and addressed herself directly to Kalter. "I remember you were always outside the group, Klaus. You never wanted to join in the discussions. You never wrote anything. Some-times we wondered why you risked yourself."

Kalter felt a surge of anger. It seemed quite extraordinary that this woman, having run away from the harsh conse-quences of her beliefs, should now be patronising him.

"Everyone has his reason," he said coldly. "What of it?"

"But we had the same reason," she insisted.

"Let's not argue, please," Guenter interrupted quickly.

"What about this American?" Kalter said, pleased to be able to come to the point. "You've watched him?"

Guenter nodded, his expression not only serious but a little unhappy, as if to indicate how much they had compromised themselves.

"Nearly every day. But some days, you understand, he stayed in his apartment. Then it was difficult."

Kalter produced the newspaper cutting.

"Does he still look like this?"

Monika studied the photograph briefly and with apparent disinterest.

"Yes. Just a little older perhaps. But, yes. Like that."

"And what has he been doing?"

"Nothing," Guenter replied. "We follow him for a bit but he does nothing. Sometimes, in the afternoons, he goes to the cinema, then to a cafe, always by himself. Other times he visits a bookshop or just walks around a park. One time he spent three hours sitting on a bench and looking at the lake. Monika came back freezing."

"Does he have visitors?"

"No."

"Have you a photograph of where he lives?"

Monika fetched her bag, opened it and produced a selection of polaroid snapshots. Some showed the house in Hans Place, others Hoffman himself, either emerging from the doorway or walking down the tree-lined avenues of a park. They had been taken at a distance and the American's features remained indistinct, though recognisable.

"Good," Kalter said, pocketing the snaps. "What about a car?"

"A dark green BMW he never uses. It's parked outside the house, in the square, registration JTL 794P."

"I'll go there this evening, to look. Does he go out at night?"

"Sometimes, just to walk, or to the cinema. Usually he stays in. You can see the light from his window on the second floor."

"So there's no routine?"

"No. Except boredom. We think he's waiting for some-thing."

Kalter suppressed a malicious grin but said nothing.

"I think you have something for me," he said finally.

"Ah, yes. Yes."

Guenter disappeared into another room that Kalter guessed was the kitchen. He came back shortly carrying a small object wrapped in a thick, oil-stained cloth. Kalter unwrapped the object with interest, folding back the cloth as though it contained a porcelain figure, something delicate and breakable. Guenter watched him nervously.

"It was the best we could do, Klaus. It was difficult. You understand? Not knowing anyone, not wanting to . . . We found a man in . . ."

"I don't want to know, Guenter," Kalter interrupted sharply. "What business is it of mine? But this . . ." And he held the gun up between two fingers, rocking it to and fro contemptuously. "A Webley!"

"I know, Klaus," Guenter said unhappily. "But what could we do? It's not been fired. Surely . . ."

Kalter laid the .38 back on top of the cloth on his knee and wiped his hands clean. He had expected something a little better than an old World War II pistol, an antique. Yet why, he reflected sourly, had he ever expected anything better from these people? He re-wrapped the gun and the six loose bullets in the oil cloth and then placed them in his briefcase.

Monika, standing with her back to the blocked-up fireplace, watched him closely. Little spots of anger had appeared on her pale cheeks.

"You have no right to complain," she burst out suddenly, ignoring her husband's agitated glance. "Why should we do it anyway? I told Guenter not to. I said it was all finished for us. Why should we get mixed up in this killing? It doesn't matter who this American is, what he has done. We have our own lives now." Kalter noticed, with distaste, that she had begun to cry. He stood up briskly.

"No," the woman persisted, brushing the tears away with her fingers. "You don't care. You don't care about Guenter's hand. Anything. And you don't understand it's over, for everyone. All of them are dead, or in jail. Everything's spoiled. What is left now? Nothing. Nothing. Nothing . . . except to live in peace. Now, when everything's over, you put us in danger again."

Kalter turned away, went towards the door, still hearing her soft blubbering behind him. Guenter stopped him apologetically.

"I'm sorry," he said. "Try and understand. It's many years since we came to England. Monika tries to forget what happened."

"Do you think they ever watch you?" Kalter wondered.

"No. Not now. Why should they? We were still legal. And it's many years now. We live very quietly."

"But they had your photograph."

Guenter shrugged.

"They had everybody's. It was all the same."

"Not mine," Kalter said spitefully, turning the knob. He sensed the other's hesitation, felt his arm grasped to prevent his leaving.

"Yes."

"Yes what?" Kalter disengaged his arm brusquely.

"Your photograph too, of course."

Momentarily surprised, despite everything, Kalter smiled nonetheless as he opened the door.

"Of course," he said evenly, shutting it behind him.

21

That night, if he had wanted to, Hoffman could have seen his killer strolling with the apparent ease of a late-season tourist around the small, locked park in the centre of Hans Place, stopping to gaze up, with no more than sincere curiosity, at his lighted window. As it was, unnoticed in the quiet, almost deserted streets, Kalter made two complete tours of the square before walking slowly back to his hotel, just another anonymous, raincoated figure in the London landscape, collar turned up against the harsh, buffeting wind.

Hoffman himself could hear it, shaking down the last dry and brittle leaves from the dark trees, bringing a promise of rain. It decided him against going out, though as usual there was nowhere to go. He was tired of London and wanted to go home, to Boston, the only place in his wandering life that had ever felt like home. Yet he would have to continue waiting. There had still been no communication from his paymasters in America, although after delivering his letter to the Embassy he had received an unexpected call from Roberts. The older man had said little beyond expressing a certain surprise that Hoffman had found disingenuous. He had even detected, if not sympathy exactly, then a kind of mild approval behind the other's words. Nevertheless Roberts had frankly admitted that the matter could not rest with him, that it was being considered elsewhere and that Hoffman would simply have to await the result of those protracted deliberations. They might, after all, he suggested, find reason to offer Hoffman some inducement to stay on. They had often hinted at his utility.

But that, too, sounded inauthentic, a conventional lie.

Hoffman had probed for information about the Beirut operation. As he might have expected, none was forthcoming, and Roberts had made a veiled allusion to their previous conversation. There were, after all, some things that do not bear looking into too deeply. Roberts had not pretended a larger ignorance, but had simply made it clear that, things being as they were, Hoffman was no longer in a position to demand clarification. For hadn't he, after all, just resigned his responsibilities?

Later, though not for the first or last time, Hoffman had gone over the whole episode in his mind step by step. There was by now little doubt that, with the premature withdrawal of the Christian troops the operation had failed. The mercenaries, one way or the other, would also have been massacred. He still felt sure that word would somehow have got back to him if this had not been the case. And Sneiger, too, was undoubtedly dead.

He thought about the boxes, remembering Roberts' evasive answers. The boxes had seemed throughout to hold the key, to have insisted on their own importance. He had never known but he had suspected, investing them with all the power of revelation. And at first Roberts' tantalising evasions, his secrecy, had confirmed that value, a value beyond money and human life, beyond the ability of one beurocrat to explain. Hoffman had wanted to know, to put his own value on the closeted secret. As if he had been reading some paperback novel, he had wanted a sense of an ending, a revelation, even a surprise — to have come full circle.

Now he had stopped wanting. The importance of the boxes had suddenly diminished, at first inexplicably and then reasonably. In some respects Roberts had said enough. He had told him what mattered that the boxes contained political secrets — "just letters". Whatever governments or individuals those "letters" compromised, whatever arrangements, plots or private agreements they revealed, they remained "just letters", in the realm of the practical and the expedient, the petty world of political machinations and manoeuvres. In other words their secrets were banal, disappointing, deeply obvious. There was no real mystery, just the trappings of one, the necessary elaborations that went with some abstract notion of national security.

Mysteries, even in novels, were always so, for how could the revelation ever live up to the expectation, the hidden promise, the secretive whispers of conspirators? Once revealed, all mysteries are banal and boring — no more than we expected. What is it ever, in novels, but a Nazi plot, a flying saucer, or a bastard birth? The fascination lies on the periphery, with the human drama, the search rather than the discovery. What were the letters to Hoffman? Nothing. In that underworld of agents and terrorists, political friends and corrupt advantages, gunmen and gangsters — what was another plot? How could it possibly have any value beyond money and human life? Its only value lay in it being a secret. The mystery would persist only until the boxes were opened, the contents known, the trivial arrangements come to light, for such mysteries are transitory and shallow and disappointing.

Hoffman's sense of an ending, his desire to know, was not real, had nothing to do with the way things worked, but was simply fictional and artificial. It was something he was just beginning to understand and appreciate. There was, as Roberts had said, no reason for him to know anything, and indeed nothing for him to know. The political world into which, for a while, he had been subtly invited knew nothing of endings and resolutions; its characteristic problems were never solved but merely alleviated; like an endless game in which the rules were constantly being changed there was only a shifting advantage and never a decisive judgement. And so it would go on for ever, eternally repetitive, never finished, played out between board and barrack room against the background of a map of Europe.

Contemplating the futility of his own past, Hoffman had thus dismissed history as a shallow trick, a game for entrepreneurs. During his long and lonely walks he had decided many things and come to many conclusions, and had found within himself, for the first time, a sense of guilt that seemed, in some fierce and biting way, to require atonement. But at least that guilt was something firm and solid and personal; it seemed to make him real and visible, seemed to underpin and explain a part of the personality he had always been separated from by the cold bright mirror of his vanity. He had never before felt remorse for anything, had never before experienced regret or shame or that common desire to begin again, to undo the mistakes, to have a second chance. To have those feelings, ironically enough, was his measure of how far he had re-entered the living stream of common experience, and in his deliberate solitude he relished them, just as once he more enjoyed the sense of casting a substantial shadow.

Lying back now, on the quilted bed in the dimly lit room, he recalled the faces of Davis and Tippett and Christie, all of them dead for no reason, almost by his own hand. He regretted it. It was part of a guilt he would always carry. To imagine it wasn't altogether his fault, to recognise how little his contribution had always been, did not justify his actions. Sneiger had worked for others, and had gulled him. Hoffman knew nothing of the value of the papers — he knew nothing at all. Yet still he agreed and participated, and put himself in the way of the blame. Ignorance was never innocence, and he had never been blind to the difference.

Hoffman closed his eyes. The past was like a film running endlessly behind them, casting up stray, half-forgotten images. He wanted, more then ever, to remember everything, not to escape anything. He had always moved ceaselessly away from the past, sloughing it off easily, but now he wished only to remember, retain, accumulate, accept. In some ways that was it: the need to accept what he was and what he had done. How readily he had always excused himself and pretended that ambition meant change and change again. He had thought himself clever and elusive, like an image out of focus. He had never accepted that he was what he did.

Hoffman fell into a heavy, troubled sleep.

22

The following day, still using the assumed name which appeared on his forged passport, Kalter hired a small saloon car and by telephone made a reservation for a double room (he was habitually optimistic) at a small hotel in South Wales. His original plan had been to stay with the Meyers after the assignment had been carried out, but having met them again he had changed his mind. In any case it would be a good opportunity to explore an apparently delightful area, and it would be safer than staying in London.

Prudence, however, was almost always a secondary consideration for Kalter. Perhaps that was something he had inherited from others in the movement, for despite their efforts to form small, self-contained revolutionary cells, and despite their insistence on rigorous planning, they were still prone to operate with the reckless opportunism which had characterised the early stages of their campaign. There was a bizarre conjuncture of covert skills and absurd bravado, so that although many had died stupidly others had succeeded in bringing off the most extraordinary coups right under the noses of a vigilant authority. Wit and imagination, coincidence and chance had often worked in their favour where the best-laid plans would have failed them. And, as Kalter knew from experience, it was one thing to suppose the presence, behind every dramatic action, of the most meticulous arrangements and quite another to be involved with the hazards and curious exigencies of real life.

Nevertheless, Kalter had already formulated his plans, had

set a time and place for Hoffman's liquidation. For the next day, then, he would have to be more careful and circumspect, less easily seduced by the sensual blandishments of London town. In the mirror, he even noticed that the black roots were beginning to show under the blond dye — and decided to do something about it promptly. He would try, he told himself, to play his role with more conviction, with more sincerity. Just because all the police forces in the world were stupid didn't, after all, excuse him from being reasonably careful. So far there was nothing to worry about — unless, of course, they were still screening the Meyers, which seemed after so many years highly unlikely. But after the murder . . .? It rather depended on Hoffman's celebrity. If he was regarded, in certain circles, as an important figure whose death could be interpreted as politically motivated then, naturally, there would be the usual hue and cry followed by an intensive police operation. In those circumstances, unless he got out quickly, there was a fair likelihood of detection. In a strange country there was no real possibility of going underground (as he could have done in Berlin) and every effort he made to avoid identification — like stealing fresh cars or travelling to remoter areas — would only attract attention and suspicion.

On the other hand, there was no reason to assume anything of the sort about Hoffman. He was a banker, that much Kalter knew, and banking is nearly always a discreet occupation. Hoffman probably operated behind the scenes, ruthlessly but quietly, and no doubt his lack of celebrity was his primary asset. Moreover, from what he had learned about the man from the Meyer's, it almost seemed as though someone had put him out to grass. If Hoffman was really a significant figure, why on earth was he just wandering around London parks by himself, looking bored? Of course he might be "waiting for something" as they had suggested, but again people in his position wouldn't normally occupy the waiting hours in idle and aimless pursuits. And yet he was important enough to be killed, and that much Kalter also knew. Important enough to be singled out by some invisible hand, but not important enough to be visibly protected, or to regard himself as a possible target.

Kalter weighed up the paradoxes. On the whole he remained convinced (and such had been his original assumption) that Hoffman's death, though it wouldn't pass unnoticed, wouldn't at the same time excite that much attention as a political crime. He was a fly in someone's ointment, but hardly as substantial a target as Drenkman or Lorenz. The symbolism was missing, that was the point. No obvious symbolic value could attach itself to the man's demise; the motive would remain cloudy, ambiguous, uncertain. In the end someone — the Palestinians, perhaps — might claim responsibility, but even that was doubtful. This killing looked more pragmatic, as if in effecting it he was doing a practical favour. And so much for that . . .

In his hotel room Kalter examined and took apart the gun. He was not a great technical expert, though he knew his way around, and he was only concerned that the weapon had not been tampered with in any way. He could have wished for enough time to test it, but of course that was impossible. He was sure the gun and its user would both prove reliable.

He also bleached his hair again — removing the tell-tale dark roots.

Kalter noticed the unmarked blue Jaguar, for the first time, just below the tube station at Belsize Park. In his driving mirror, as he overtook a lorry moving down Haverstock Hill, he saw it pull out recklessly behind him and heard the complaining horns of cars going in the other direction. He slowed down to accommodate its further progress but, braking sharply, the Jaguar merely tucked itself in behind the small Escort and followed it sheepishly into Camden, then along Hampstead Road.

Lower down, in the congested traffic of the West End, he lost it again, and thought little of it. His suspicion had simply been instinctive and reflexive, perhaps irrational, and afterwards — as he drove steadily along the Embankment, past the Tate Gallery, towards Chelsea — it even caused him a feeling of self-approach. It was almost as if the gun, nestling in the glove compartment just in front of him, had given him a new and unwanted self-consciousness, heightening his senses.

Kalter had gone, that morning, to walk on the Heath, that strange, residual area of greenery, with its copses and ponds, that stretched between Hampstead and Highgate. He had arrived early, and apart from a few individuals exercising their dogs had seen, once he reached the heart of the landscape, nobody.

He had walked for two hours, then he had gone back to the car, suddenly cold and bored and strangely irritated by the placid English scene.

Three hours later he was eating a light lunch — nothing more than fish — in a Chelsea restaurant that turned out to be full of young French students, boisterous, bad-mannered and well-dressed. He kept an eye on the clock, a large and ugly reproduction, fixed to the wall over the long, well-stocked bar. It was now twelve thirty. Hoffman had usually left his apartment by now, if only to go on one of his aimless journeys. Yesterday he had visited the Natural History Museum; the day before, in the damp drizzle, the Serpentine. He was not difficult to follow. He was like a man, Kalter decided, who had suffered a recent bereavement that went too deep for tears but removed all purpose.

His manner was abstracted, remote, divided. He was unconscious of the world outside him, staring out at it, through the window of some cafe, as if its familarity puzzled and disturbed him. There was something insubstantial, elusive about his presence; something temporary and fragile. Against that, Kalter felt his own reality as emphatically as though it had been stamped out of tin: hard at the edges, solid, permanent.

Hoffman would normally return by mid-afternoon, and then stay in his rooms for the rest of the day.

The clock moved on to the hour. Kalter called across the waiter and paid his bill, leaving a modest tip. The waiter hardly had time to notice him with all the commotion; one of the students stood on his chair and was noisily pulled down by others.

On the pavement outside Kalter stopped to look at a girl waiting beside an occupied telephone box. She was wearing a bright raincoat and boots and holding an umbrella, tilted back slightly so that he would see the whole of her face without shadow. She stared back at him prettily, immodestly, and for a moment he thought of going over. In two days time he would be away from all this, in Wales, otherwise by himself. He hesitated. The girl approached him, confidently smiling, asking if he had change for the telephone.

"Sure," Kalter said. He fumbled in his trouser pocket, observed by blue eyes rimmed black. "No. Sorry."

"Oh, well. Never mind. I have some anyway." She pouted, smiled, stayed where she was. She was younger than he had thought, perhaps only nineteen. Behind her confidence there was a detectable, nervous reticence, a shyness, as if she came from a class that did not approach men openly but usually waited. Now, it seemed, she had nothing else to say, nothing prepared, mechanical. Kalter wondered what lonely, sudden impulse had caused her to precipitate this awkwardness. She started to turn away.

"I'm sorry," he said.

She turned back, almost puzzled.

"Sorry?"

"About the money."

"Oh!" She laughed, nervously but with relief.

Kalter pressed home his advantage, liking her, even the crusty English manner.

"Would you like some coffee?"

"I don't . . ." She pouted again, looked away, her deliberations comic somehow and self-conscious. Eventually, with possible reluctance, she shook her head. "I couldn't," she said. "Really I couldn't."

"I don't understand." Kalter persisted, playing his part.

"Pardon?"

"I don't understand why you say 'couldn't' like that. You mean you don't want to?"

"No, I . . ."

"I suppose you have something better to do," he remarked with a grin.

"No, really, it isn't that at all." Ridiculously honest, too, her class. "I've nothing to do, actually. I was thinking of catching the train back home . . . in about an hour."

"Good," Kalter said.

"I'm sorry?"

"I mean you have time for a coffee. I could drive you to the station then."

"Well . . ." She looked him over again with tentative approval, "All right. Where?"

Her manner had become brisk, sharp, assertive. Kalter thought he might not like her after all.

There was a small, old-fashioned tea shop not far from his hotel. They sat at a table near the bay window and Melinda ordered a pot of tea for two.

Melinda's father was a retired army officer, her mother was dead. The family had a house near Brighton and another in Southern Ireland. They bred horses and entertained politicians. They were "well off" rather than rich, and were rather remotely connected to the Duke of Kent. Melinda herself was looking, without a great deal of enthusiasm, for a job.

"I was thinking of something in publishing," she said, daintily holding the little china cup, "but I've decided it would be awfully boring."

Kalter repressed the inclination to point out that her entire life seemed awfully boring, from the moment she'd been given her first pony to the time she went up to Oxford.

"Now I think I might try the magazines." She shook her head. "Mind you, I don't even know if I could *stand* to live in London.

"You're German aren't you?" Her observations appeared indiscriminate, following each other at random.

"Austrian, I was born in Vienna. My father was German."

"How lovely! I went ski-ing there last winter. I wanted to go again but then mummy died suddenly." She stared down, briefly, at the crisp white table cloth.

"I'm sorry," Kalter said conventionally.

"No, it's alright. I'm over it now. Can we go for a walk, please, Michael?"

They left the tea shop and walked slowly to the Chelsea Embankment, past Carlyle's house, through the Edwardian streets. Melinda continued to talk about herself as if this was the only topic in which she had any interest. Kalter heard about the neighbours in Ireland, the recent and "awful" argument with her boyfriend (Kalter could imagine him in jodhpurs and boots), her trips to Africa, Egypt, Beirut, her fondness for Paris, her dislike of Rome.

"The men in Rome," she said with a slight shudder, "are horrible! Just chauvinists. They look at you all the time and then follow you. Sometimes I was very frightened."

"Yes. I can imagine."

They stopped and looked over at the boatyard. The water was scummy and escaping oil had given it a greasy surface. The houseboats rocked gently against their moorings, green plants in the windows, domestic curtains. Kalter was struck with the absurdity of his situation, this strange conjunction of the ordinary — a man and woman leaning against a wall on a dull Wednesday afternoon — and the historic. In a few hours, tomorrow, on another dreary afternoon he would be ending a life, putting a bullet through a skull. Now he was trying to think up ways of discarding this embarrassing girl, still fluting away in her high, stiff, colourless voice and actually putting her shoulder to his. She was looking for some protection against the brutal vicissitudes of a world in which you could lose the affection of men called Roger or Nigel. And that was the fullest measure of her parochialism, just as everything else about her reflected the blank stupidity of her class.

"Beirut was my favourite city," she explained. "We only stayed a week — Daddy was doing some business — but it

194

was so different and colourful. Very beautiful."

"Not now," Kalter said.

"No. I don't think so. Have you ever been to the Middle East?"

"Yes." He almost wanted to tell her: yes, actually, that's where I was taught to shoot and handle explosives; that's where they sent me; that's where I was trained to be what I am.

She didn't ask him where. She was always less interested in his answers than in her own questions, those formal declarations of her own interests.

They walked on. It was four o'clock. Already the streets were darker, the cold evening descending like a fog.

"I've missed my train," she announced.

It annoyed him. She was no more than a girl, playing games.

"I'll run you to the station in my car," he said tersely.

When he looked he saw she was pouting, and there was an unpleasantly sincere expression in her eyes. She was trying to appear vulnerable, helpless, in need of his attention and support. But suddenly she gave a little, excited, conspiratorial grin.

"I'd like to take you for dinner," she said. "Will you let me?"

"I have to see someone in an hour," he replied flatly, not welcoming the arm that had sneaked boldly but inevitably through his.

"Oh, in an hour!" She giggled. "I mean later. You could meet me there. I have some shopping to do, anyway."

"What about your train?"

"There's one every hour. Anyway, I can always go back tomorrow. I said I might."

Kalter hesitated. She had somehow managed to surprise him. Yet he remembered the Englishwoman in Paris, the failed promises. In any case he didn't like the girl. She was an empty little vessel, a prig, a lost child. What he wanted . . .

"Yes," he said. "Alright. Where?"

She gave him the name of a Russian restaurant just off Brompton Road. He had passed it once.

"Eight?"

He nodded.

"I think I'll take a taxi to Oxford Street."

He saw her into the taxi and she waved to him through the small back window. Then he hailed one himself, went back to Chelsea to collect his car and drove through the building traffic towards Knightsbridge. This time it was not a Jaguar but an ordinary and quite old-looking Cortina. It seemed to follow him as he laced his way through the familiar back streets, though sometimes it remained two or three cars behind. He couldn't be sure. To be safe, however, he altered his route, turned away from Knightsbridge and went north. After three sets of traffic lights the trailing car had disappeared.

Nevertheless, he abandoned the idea of going back to Hans Place. There was little point anyway, he told himself, just to see that feeble light at the window. Come tomorrow, he would simply take his chances. And if not tomorrow, well, the next day. And if he didn't kill Hoffman? So what. He would lose money and a little credibility, but nothing more. The Meyers were probably right; the movement wasn't going to last forever. It was cracking at the seams — and it would take something more spectacular than this common killing to revive it. This, more and more, had the appearance of nothing but a special favour. So who was to blame him if he left the wretched little man alive?

He arrived at the restaurant, deliberately late, at half past the hour. The single room was crowded but Melinda had already secured a corner table and a drink and was examining her nails. She gave him a frozen stare that was no more than fleeting, obligatory, then smiled as he took off his coat and sat down beside her on one of the plain wooden chairs. She had changed and he noticed that the new dress not only softened her outline but made her look older. She had also unfastened her blond hair and let it fall freely, in its luxuriant thickness, around her face. He nevertheless doubted whether the change had transformed her in any more substantial way; it simply reinforced his earlier perception that she would make a good model — a good peg to hang clothes on.

"I was worried," she said, handing him a sheet of paper that passed as a menue. "I thought you weren't going to come."

"I'd like a drink," he said.

"And to follow it?" She gazed at him mischievously. He could make nothing of the menu.

"You order."

She did so competently, briskly, with an authority that came from dealing easily with those of a class ineluctably beneath hers. With Kalter the ease disappeared, the formal codes were scrambled. Perhaps that was why she clung. Beyond that, he was sure, she was simply after a harmless adventure, an anecdote. Her own life was pure, superior, but dull and just occasionally she required some excitement that was not ritual, that upset the neat balance, the fond equilibrium of her entrenched and priveleged existence. An unbroken horse, a stranger, a sniff of cocaine — anything would do, as long as it wasn't real.

The food arrived.

"Did you have a good meeting?"

"Yes, thank you."

23

When he woke, very early as usual, it was to find her still sleeping, curled up on the other side of the rumpled bed, her bent back towards him. He stroked the spine thoughtfully, feeling the sharp rill with his fingers, thinking not of her but of Hoffman, strangely amusingly excited.

He got up and went to the bathroom. When he came back she was half awake, sleepily stretching her arms, searching lazily for his warmth. He began to get dressed.

"Michael?"

"Yes?"

She sat up, her back against the mahogany head board.

"I could sleep for days."

He buttoned his shirt.

"It's early. Come back to bed. Please, it's still dark out there."

"I always get up early. Always."

Out of the corner of his eye he saw her slip from between the sheets. She kissed him, lightly, on the cheek, disappeared into the bathroom and shut the door.

"What are you going to do today?" she shouted. "Have you any plans?"

He didn't reply until she had re-emerged. "Yes, I have."

She pouted familiarly.

"That don't include me?"

Her dressing, her body were now of no interest to him. She sat primly on the edge of the bed, her lips bright with fresh lipstick.

"When are you setting off?"

"Where?"

"To Wales, silly."

"Perhaps this evening, I don't know."

She paused, playing with the fringes of the bed-cover, threading them through her long fingers.

"Would you take me with you?" She looked up shyly, timidly. He was still a stranger.

At first he didn't say anything. It had just been a preposterous idea, an expectation she hadn't met. She looked away gloomily and felt the smart of tears, the final humiliation.

"You don't want me, do you?"

"Of course you can come." He nodded his head unenthusiastically.

She clapped her hands together spontaneously and felt embarrassed immediately afterwards.

"Oh, how wonderful!" she said.

"I will collect you somewhere about six."

"Where?"

He tried to think of a suitable place, but couldn't.

"Where do you suggest?"

"Well, where will you be?"

"Outside King's Cross Station, at six."

"Perfect. It doesn't matter if you're late. I'll just wait. I'll buy some champagne for when we get there."

"Fine."

He drew back the heavy curtains and left them open. It was nearly eight o'clock and already the street was busy with people hurrying to work. A man in a dark suit, a briefcase beside him on the ground, was exploring the engine of his large, shining car. Three schoolgirls, in dark blue raincoats, paraded cheerfully down the pavement. And then there was a young man, with a beard and a heavy coat, lounging against the park railings, watching the front of the hotel, smoking a cigarette. Five minutes later he was still there, though he had turned his back and was looking into the park instead. Kalter moved away from the window.

"What are you going to do?" he asked, making an effort to be polite.

Melinda was already dressed in her red raincoat, her bag packed.

"Shopping, I suppose. Can't be bothered to look for a job. Don't want one anyway." She laughed. "How about taking me for breakfast first? I could eat a horse. I know somewhere really, really good where we can have hot croissants with ham and cheese inside. It's not far."

Dressed and made-up, ready for the public world again, her real element, she was the same brisk, authoritative self.

"Where?"

"Notting Hill Gate. We can take the car."

Kalter reluctantly found his coat. They went downstairs. In the lobby the woman at reception asked if he was checking out that day or the next. Kalter confirmed his earlier arrangement; he would be out of his room by mid-day.

That morning, Hoffman received notification by letter that he should be available for interview, in Washington, the following Monday. Reading the brief, officious note he experienced a sense of immeasurable relief. He was about to be let out of the cage.

He spent some time deliberating whether or not to wait another day before travelling back direct to Washington, but finally decided he would prefer to spend the extra time in New York rather than London. New York winters were as harsh as winters anywhere, with the winds whipping down the long avenues, but somehow they seemed less oppressive than the dampness of London, a dampness that seeped into the bones so that the chill never left them.

A telephone call to British Airways confirmed that there was no problem booking a flight for later that evening. He should book in at Heathrow airport as soon after nine o'clock as possible. He began to pack at once, not carefully as had once been his habit but quickly and sloppily, crumpling his suits, throwing shirts and shoes haphazardly into the bulging cases. He thought about New York, its friendliness and welcome, its bars and buildings, and with greater affection of Boston, the place of pilgrims, the fresh green lip of land. The idea of the journey towards it, even by modern convenience, filled him not only with anticipation but a queralous, almost childish, sense of excitement. Like the pilgrims and convicts it was a new beginning, a promise, an absurdly romantic hope. And he had pinned himself down to that — to nothing more substantial than a romantic affectation, something in truth that was foreign to the European nature but still present in the American. But what else was left? Nothing material, nothing worked-for or gained. Just a small, almost spiritual (though the word would have embarrassed him) anticipation, a romantic readiness to seek change, to go back. With the end of his hurried packing his old life, in some real sense, was over. He had sloughed off the old skin. The original man, the confident, arrogant, worldly American, the man who had flown in just a few weeks previously, was as good as dead.

Kalter had noted, outside the hotel, that the young man in his shabby coat was still there, not waiting but somehow not watching either, simply a stubborn visible presence gloating over the limited view.

Melinda continued her garrulous, one-way conversation, noticing nothing, least of all Kalter's quietness. Once in the car she turned the radio on, switching rapidly through the bands, laughing, touching his hand on the steering wheel.

"Today I'm going to have four whole croissants. I'm starving! God, look at that funny man reading his paper while he's driving."

There was heavy traffic, slowing them to a crawl. Kalter thumped the steering wheel with his hand.

"It doesn't matter, darling . . ."

A white, unmarked Rover pulled erratically in front of them, braked sharply and pulled away.

"Stupid twits," Melinda said.

"Which way?" Kalter demanded, stopping at a red light.

"Oh!" She put her hand to her face in mock dismay. "Where are we? I know. Yes. Turn . . . right at the next set of lights. Just up there. See?"

Kalter indicated for the turn.

"What about that sign?" he said.

"What sign?"

"It says Notting Hill Gate straight on. Yes?"

"No," she shook her head. "I mean, yes. I'm taking you the back way. The traffic is ghastly isn't it? Here!"

He waited for the line of lorries, belching black fumes, and cars to pass, entering the narrower street.

"There!" she said. "I told you."

The road ahead, curving gently, was almost empty. Kalter accelerated.

"When you get to the end, turn left. I think that's right."

When they arrived at the junction it was only to find their access blocked by a stream of vehicles. The white Rover pulled in behind them. In his mirror Kalter watched it reverse, back into a drive then disappear down another side street. Melinda had watched it too.

"Yes. That's a good idea. That's another way. Why don't we try that?"

Kalter repeated the proceedure, and soon caught up with the Rover, travelling so slowly that he began to pull round it. Melinda touched his hand nervously.

"I shouldn't. They might be police."

There were three men in the car, two in front and one behind. The latter, craning his neck, looked back briefly. The road ahead, apart from parked cars, was deserted. Kalter made up his mind. He indicated to overtake, began to depress the accelarator, but then he slammed the brake on so violently that the girl jolted forward, her protecting hand bashing into the windscreen. Her scream, reflexive, automatic, died abruptly.

The Rover had swerved across the road in front of them, blocking both lanes, and stopped. As Kalter watched, shifting through the gears, its doors opened and the men inside began to clamber out. He couldn't see any guns.

"What is it?" Melinda wailed. "Michael? Michael? We nearly —"

Kalter turned and started to reverse at speed down the drab street, wrestling the wheel round, slithering into an open driveway, racking the stick into first. Melinda had twisted her body sideways, away from him, one hand on the dashboard the other on the door. She was moaning softly and there was a smear of blood from an invisible cut on her cheek.

The few sparse, dying trees by the side of the road went past in a blur, like a film running too fast, clacking round the spool. Melinda shouted at him to stop, screamed again, saw the marked car with its whirling light swerve to avoid them, dizzily turning, heard the pandemonium of sirens and tyres, found herself flung against the door. They were on the wrong side of the road, squeezed between rows of traffic, brushing metal to metal. She fumbled for the door catch, her fingers stiff and clumsy, trembling. Kalter saw her and his hand came down, hitting the top of her shoulder blade, the pain jarring her neck as if a stone had crashed against it, causing her to whimper. Kalter's eyes were ferocious, with concentration and fear, she thought. But also anger. Such terrible anger . . .

"Michael . . . Michael . . ."

The wail of sirens but, behind, the blue light vanished.

"It was you," Kalter said, his voice different, harsher. "You."

"No, Michael. What?"

His hand caught her full across the face, driving her head back, bringing blood.

"You told them."

"You'll crash . . . Oh, God."

"You told them."

"What have you done?"

The blue light behind them again, somehow spinning around the car, reflected on the windows, the mad face. A red light in front.

"Michael . . .!"

"You told them. All the fucking time . . ."

"No," she said, watching spots of blood drip, drip, sticky between her fingers. "I don't know what you mean. What have you done?"

His nerve was returning, the blindness had gone. Inside he was cold and bitter and full of regrets. He undid the catch of the glove compartment letting the flap fall open. In the end, he thought, women always get you. But not this time.

A car pulled out onto the road just a hundred yards in front. He saw it in time, responded, changed down at fifty, drifted round the car and entered the street from which it had come. The street, hedged in by low terraces of red-brick houses, angled away to the left, narrowed, ended in a turning circle before a row of newer buildings. The car slewed across the road, juddering, its front end ploughing into the side of a parked car. Kalter's body slammed against the steering column; he heard the tinkle of breaking glass. His right hand closed around the butt of the pistol, drawing it out, just as the passenger door swung open. The girl had one foot on the pavement. He could see how her whole body was convulsed, how it shook absurdly. Her face, as she looked back, was as white as alabaster, her mouth hung open stupidly.

Disbelief and dazed confusion reigned supreme on the girl's face as Kalter fired the Webley at point blank range. She fell backwards onto the road, her legs at an absurd angle against the car's side. He opened his door calmly and ran behind the parked car, its side buckled to wait.

Kalter fired one shot towards the barricade of cars and ran, half-crouching towards the wall. He turned back after a few yards and regained his position behind the car. He had no idea why. For some reason he felt confused and unsure, and one impluse preceded another with strange, unnerving rapidity. It was all unreal, unprepared, unlikely. He didn't want to die. Yet it seemed inevitable. He didn't want to surrender. The girl was dead — so he couldn't.

His hands and face were sweating miserably. He felt cold

and was shivering. For some moments, watching everything about him, he felt like laughing ridiculousy. His pants were wet. He could hear, as if it came from a thousand miles away, the booming voice beckoning, seducing him out with its infinite promises. Sweet talk, he thought. Such sweet talk. He fired aimlessly at the cars, bursting a window. The blue cold and spitting steel in his hand was comforting after all. He fired again and again. The people had gone inside. Shots rattled off the wreckage, whined over his head. He rubbed the barrel of the gun against his cheek, digging it in, stood up and fired the final bullet nowhere. He was hit in the throat and head and died instantly.

24

Hoffman's plane rose steeply over London, tilting away. The city, traced in lights, glittered fetchingly below, reminding him of a dark Venetian church with its brilliant candles flickering. The plane was full of Americans, garrulous as ever, painstakingly friendly. Hoffman ordered a whisky, took out his book and settled back.

The middle-aged woman next to him, rich and happy, sparkling modestly with jewels, attempted conversation. Like other women of that generation she had lost or forsaken her own personality in favour of her husband's. Her own life was second-hand, a pale and watery reflection. So she told Hoffman, with smug, indulgent honesty that her husband, Walter Right, was going to run for the Senate.

"He's such a good man," she said, "and a good Jew. He thinks we're reneging on our commitments to Israel. He thinks this government is the worst we've ever had. He thinks, do you know, they're going in with those Palestinian people. All that talk of peace. Poppycock. He says the next thing you know we'll be letting them have Jerusalem back. Can you imagine?"

"I think it's unlikely," Hoffman replied wearily, watching the last lights go out below.

"Well, Walter says there's something going on. It should be investigated. People ought to know where they stand. We can't just stand back and let the commies take what they want. It's 'thank you very much, for this' and 'thank you very much for that', as far as they're concerned. That horrible man of theirs. We just have to let them know we mean real business. None of this talk, talk, talk. We ought to be doing everything we can, especially when it comes to Israel."

"Yes," Hoffman managed, "certainly. But it's a little complicated."

"Complicated!" She looked at him with horror. "Why? It doesn't need to be. That's what we want. Everything above board, honest and decent. That's what my husband calls responsible government."

"He sounds a very worthy man."

"Yes he is, as a matter of fact. He's an idealist. He believes in having principles and sticking to them. He believes in finding out the truth. At the moment we don't know what's going on, do we?" She sat back, temporarily satisfied.

"The truth," Hoffman muttered, more to himself. Then he looked towards her again, seeing the deep lines of encroaching age, the heavy make-up, the pompous mind. "It doesn't exist," he said clearly.

There was a folded English newspaper across her lap. He could just about see the picture — the crashed car, the two bodies. A little later, having fished out a large round pair of spectacles, the woman began reading, stopping to tap the picture with a jewelled hand.

"Shocking," she said loudly, sweeping her massive gaze round to meet Hoffman's and somehow implicating him in her contempt. "What kind of a world are we living in? Every day it's the same. What on earth is going on?" Her irritation was feverish, compulsive. "Who are all these people, anyway — the ones who cause all the trouble?"

She appeared to expect an answer. Hoffman, half-seriously, had none. He remembered a phrase.

"The armies of the night," he said softly, inadequately.

A SELECTED LIST OF WAR BOOKS
PUBLISHED BY CORGI

While every effort is made to keep prices low, it is sometimes necessary to increase prices at short notice. Corgi Books reserve the right to show new retail prices on covers which may differ from those previously advertised in the text or elsewhere.

The prices shown below were correct at the time of going to press.

ORDER FORM

All these books are available at your book shop or newsagent, or can be ordered direct from the publisher. Just tick the titles you want and fill in the form below.

CORGI BOOKS, Cash Sales Department, P.O. Box 11, Falmouth, Cornwall.

Please send cheque or postal order, no currency.

Please allow cost of book(s) plus the following for postage and packing:

U.K. Customers—Allow 45p for the first book, 20p for the second book and 14p for each additional book ordered, to a maximum charge of £1.63.

B.F.P.O. and Eire—Allow 45p for the first book, 20p for the second book plus 14p per copy for the next 7 books, thereafter 8p per book.

Overseas Customers—Allow 75p for the first book and 21p per copy for each additional book.

NAME (Block Letters) ....

ADDRESS ....

....